DONALD SMITH is a renowned of the Scottish Storytelling Cent wright and theatre producer. He was also a founding Director of the National Theatre of Scotland, for which he campaigned over a decade. Born in Glasgow of Irish parentage, Donald Smith was brought up in Scotland, immersed in its artistic and cultural life. Smith's non-fiction includes *Storytelling Scotland: A Nation in Narrative, God, the Poet and the Devil: Robert Burns and Religion* and *Arthur's Seat: Journeys and Evocations*, co-authored with Stuart McHardy. His *Freedom and Faith* provides an insightful long-term perspective on the ongoing Independence debate, while *Pilgrim Guide to Scotland* recovers the nation's sacred geography. Donald Smith is currently Director of Tracs (Traditional Arts and Culture Scotland), based at the Storytelling Centre.

STORM AND SHORE

A Bardsaga

DONALD SMITH

Luath Press Limited

EDINBURGH

www.luath.co.uk

For Naomi Mitchison
Cailleach nan Sgeulachdan

First published 2022

ISBN: 978-1-80425-035-8

The author's right to be identified as author of this book under the
Copyright, Designs and Patents Act 1988 has been asserted.

Printed and bound by Clays Ltd., Bungay

Typeset in 10.5 point Sabon by Lapiz

Acknowledgements

THE ART OF landscape evoked in *Storm and Shore*, though not the character of Lucy Salter, is partly inspired by the work of Skye-based artist Julie Brook, who lived for a period of months on the uninhabited Hebridean island of Mingulay. There amidst other works she created fire beacons in the intertidal zone. However any other resemblance between any fictional character in this story and any living person is accidental. Historical figures mentioned are viewed solely through the perceptions of the characters.

Acknowledgements

LANDFALL

LONG AND SHALLOW *and far away; unroll me like a map.*

On one side run narrow straits of sea. Wind crested. On the other, sea loch reaches like an extended finger. Making almost an island.

People come here to escape, from whatever you need to escape.

At the top there is a village and sheltered harbour. And to the west on the sea side a landing place.

Below that a wide sandy bay extends, closed off at the southern end by a rocky arm that points seaward. And in that bay an island. Sanctuary Bay. Beyond the arm, on both sides, stony shorelines run below rough muirland.

The cowled ones came here for refuge. Later the drovers made a track from sea to loch, a respite from the cattle boats or fearful salty plunges, water thrashing, eyes distended.

Once the roads were all at sea; this peninsula, the landfall. No-one has to come this way now.

I am faraway; but sanctuary still.

ONE

GIVING ME SPACE, right. But did they mean this small?

Two wee rooms, and a kitchen that must have been a byre. Everything mucked in together – beast and man.

Hearth deep in the gable; old enough. Walls like a fort, stone-flagged floor. It's a new roof though, and all mod cons installed, even a hob. In case the aliens land, like me.

Himself from the village does not seem to approve anyway. Tall, upright old fella, looking me up and down like a dubious recruit. White beard, beak of a nose and eyes from the sea. Maybe the owner.

Inspection complete, Mr MacLean leaves me to it. Well, I can find him at the landing stage beyond the village, if necessary. That famous Highland hospitality.

And another first night for me. Nothing new there, though strange in the stone of it – the age like home. But definitely not like there. Nothing like there. So unpack; eat tinned food, hob-warmed drink, turn in early to bed hopefully.

One fifty-eight. Observation dies hard, even with the sweats.

Much the same: huts roofless, thorn enclosures smoking, clothes and pots scattered, everyday trashed. In this version, I seem to be counting, turning them over to identify age and sex. More and more. Someone's shouting to leave, go quick, quicker. One brightly coloured figure, stretched in a doorway.

I turn it, pulling; her arm comes away in my hand. The head shoots up and falls from her shoulders. Running on the drop, suddenly awake.

Somewhere light seeps in, more than the clock. Drag myself to the window and stare out. Starlight, layer after layer, into night, till my head swims and subsides. No sky have I seen like that since leaving Africa.

Pull on clothes to go out but realise I am shivering. Back under the covers, turning between fitful sleeps. Another test failed. Counting towards another day.

I come to with a dry mouth, and even the tea tastes rancid. Sooner I can cut back on sweeties the better.

Bit shaky on the pins, but get out to try the air, get my bearings. But don't look; there's no need, no warning signs, no danger. Still.

Listen; shut your eyes and listen. Gulls wheeling. Terns somewhere. Feel some wind on the cheek. And waves plashing on the shore, like you could wait forever on the next one. Nothing. Nothing else. Something chugging – boat far out. Fishing maybe beyond the bay, on an open sea.

You can look now. Take the view west. Islay, Jura, Tiree, Ireland, and all the waves between. So I'm told, but today everything's shifting grey. Melting, merging somehow. Irish air.

Except down there, right below, the shore – my beach. A wide sandy strip runs clear as a bell to the rocky point, enclosing its little island. That's the spot for me, down to the sea, all laid out beneath.

My first wee stroll.

Here I go then. There's an old yard behind the cottage, cobbled. 'Causie' they used to call this at home. Few tumbled walls, then the path. Left to the church further on, which needs checked out; right back to the village; left and hard right for the shore. It's like spaghetti junction for sheep. Not a human in sight. The legs are working fine, just watch the feet shifting one in front of the other.

Few last hummocks, then a drop. Mini-cliff tucked in on the edge; wee surprise for the unwary. But not for me, not at all. Wait though, there's steps, aligned with the path; they've been cut into the rock. How long have they been here?

Well-worn footsteps. I am on the sand. And a smirr of fine rain blows in. First day of the holiday. Take it on the cheek, cool.

Wan sun rinsed out by six o'clock. Light slants onto beach, into tent and cave mouth. But this rising is obscured, aborted by low cloud, riding in on a light breeze as the tide goes back. Grey... blue... watercolour black.

A jacket is needed on top of my trousers and jersey to walk the tideline. Boots as well.

Plastic debris, a nylon net, rope, wood, washed out and smoothed down. I gather one piece of timber striated and blackened at the end as if it had been burnt. No fires aboard ship surely. Observe, don't imagine.

Today's tasks:

Sketch the island under cloud – might become a series in gouache.

Photograph the sheep's skull uncovered yesterday at high tide. What interventions might suit?

Record the variations in sand cover... like hour glasses?

Go back along the point to observe the different kinds of seaweed on rock. Check tidal deposits.

May see more seals. How do they fit into these cycles? Are they an intervention?

Must go to the shop and get dry matches. Call in at Mr MacLean's for any post. Return along the north beach to my bay and view the declining light from an indirect perspective.

It is surprising how quickly the evenings are already earlier here. Should I go to bed earlier as well to maximise the daylight hours? How many more hours of sleep can I absorb? And stay alert.

Must allow more time to record and reflect. Expand this journal. The clues are here as well as out there – all in the looking.

The key is beneath the mat. The latch is fastened on the outside of the inside door. The nurse knows where to look if she needs to gain admittance, and I am still away.

She cannot be harming herself in any way she might try. The delivery van is late again with the boats all landed, and a fine catch. Why should the fishermen have to pay for their mistakes if the crabs and lobsters are not in their best condition? The estate has its landing fees and there is my commission. That may be the van now. Let them sort it out amongst themselves.

One day there may be nothing except pleasure craft here, moored at the lochside. What shall I have then but the croft? Poor land.

Ewan's sheep are over the brow of the hill. They like to come down on the old rigs for the grass, but not today. And there is no sign of the lame yow. She is broken, and the crows will be having her. I have no need now to be working this ground. Ewan will give me a lamb or two. To think on the people struggling up here from the shore with creels of seaweed to mulch these stones. You can see the nettle beds yet. They set down their loads long since, and lay down in the earth, or left for other lands. Leaving us to remain.

There now the lark is rising. You think she would be used by now to my walking. There has been no-one on the ridge today. Except the fox, he has left his mark. On patrol, watching his chance to kill. He will be home now over the brae. Rutting with his bitch.

The clouds are off the sea today, carrying a soft cover of rain. Enough, though, to put the beasts on the lee side.

But the artist lady is out at her scavenging. She tells me that she is after anything the sea will give. Dulse, tangle, driftwood, torn nets, the broken ends of fish boxes. They are all plastic now. Perhaps she is not wholly well in her own mind, yet she appears clear enough. She looked me directly in the eye when she asked for permission to camp by the cave mouth. Strange for a woman on her own, but there are letters and phone calls in the village.

Next she will be meeting our new Irishman. Someone else made the booking for him, or I would have realised ahead of the time. Why is he coming here with that name on him? Perhaps he is ignorant of his own kind and their history.

Afternoons are worst when the wee jobs tail off. Too early for the telly, especially if you don't have one.

Not having a drink either, not yet.

Radio Scotland Newsdrive, 4.30m, Radio Four PM, 5.00pm. Foreign news to be taken in small doses.

Electric bars switched off in an empty fireplace. Only September after all. Scottish September.

Woman on the beach seemed interesting. But too busy to talk, or unwilling. An art project of some sort – personal thing, cutting off other questions, as if art wouldn't be my bag. Has me down as fisherman, or lonely alkie. First impressions. Like I had trespassed on her private shoreline. Fair enough. It's all about territory, so they say. I'm here now as well. For a while anyroads.

Could spread everything out on the kitchen table, dining table. Not required otherwise. Space for notes, briefings, photos, maps, e-mails. All packed and ready.

Or stash them in the press for a rainy day. Neat piles folded like sheets. Not why I'm supposed to be here, but is there anything else to do?

A single-storied house, white harled, sits above the landing place. This is the one. Only these bouldered outhouses remember when people were forced down from more fertile ground to the sea. And before that.

No-one about. Pass through the first door and raise the latch. A bowed white-haired figure by the hearth. Smell of old-fashioned peats. The white hair is cropped to the neck.

The skin is brown-weathered, folded. Round shouldered in a cardigan she sits and stares at the smouldering embers.

A kettle hangs above the fire, gently beginning to steam. Is this her way of inviting me, calling me in? I know I shall be made welcome in her place.

Better out even if it is raining. Soft like autumn on the Foyle. This path seems to run all the way along the spine of the ridge. North to the village with branches off to the beach. Due south, through sparse conifers to the church and headland beyond. End of the line.

Just getting my bearings when old MacLean comes stalking out from the trees. Is he spying on me? Paranoia.

Hopes I have everything needed for my comfort? No problem, short of any normal neighbourly chat. Hard to discuss the weather when it's so clearly in your face, for the next while anyway.

His eyes are light grey, or some kind of blue, cold and piercing like a hawk. Not much round here these lenses miss. Then he marches off – sentry on his beat, periscopes revolving. Thinks the Russians are still coming, or the Taliban. No native rebels anyroads, not now they have their own parliament, their own gripey wee Stormont. Hell mend them.

What's her highness of the beach up to? Check it out from the top of the bank; no call to be interrupting at this late stage of the day. Nearly time for refreshments.

Does she actually sleep in that wee tent? Trust someone to drag a tent into it. Sand everywhere, but not that kind of sand. Bloody hell, with not a drop to drink.

The island stands out in focus, very clear compared to the soft grey forms behind. But when you begin to sketch, you realise that is a trick of the light. All the edges are blurred to differing degrees. It would work for watercolours or a crayon, not acrylics.

I set off back along the beach towards the point which MacLean calls the seal rocks. They form the southern end of the bay, as if at one time they reached out to touch the island. Now the sea flows in forced by a strong current between the big islands and this peninsula. Nearly an island. Depending on the tides I suppose.

And those tides bring in the boulders, casting them up even on the southern side of the bay. I don't understand how that happens unless the tides spiral round. Hidden strength and power.

To a casual eye, the beach merges imperceptibly into a rocky shore, that then piles cumulatively, erratically towards the southern point. But I only saw that properly today, seeing for the first time. There is a distinct frontier, a boundary of stones which marks the transition. Looking and not discerning.

First, I sketched it rapidly on the ground, trying to capture the actual moment of perception. Then I photographed the boundary from a variety of angles, near and distant.

Next, I started to build a mini-wall, a partial divider on one section of the beach. As if the Romans, or the Celts here, had constructed a fortified frontier; then time and weather had broken it down, leaving only intermittent sections standing. I used broken boulders from higher up, where they pretend to have always been stones. I am layering like a drystone dyker, or a medieval mason working from rough foundations.

Finally, I sketched and photographed the wall in its unfinished state. These images could be the basis of some paintings relating the traverse textures of the shore between sand and stone, to the up and down tidal flows. You can see that in the debris or the sand patterns though only for a short time as the next movements take hold. Unceasing natural energies, which everything from alluvial grains to monumental rocks contain. The passage of time but also cyclical, recurrent.

Or it could be a cultural energy as if the whole landscape is a broken-down form of history. Big words – keep focussed on the work.

This has been a productive day. I am moving closer to the patterns I want to reflect, to keep pace with. A bit closer. As I went to-and-fro with my stones, I could see more seal activity on the headland. New arrivals perhaps following some pattern of their own.

So much to understand. I am putting a step into the dance, letting the mind go.

Darkness over the land. Below the starlight speckled surface of the sea, the country of seals. Finding the depths, propulsing tirelessly through undersea glimmer, bulls journey to their ancestral breeding grounds. Remote, sea-pounded outposts.

For now, cows still gather, shuffling and moaning on more sheltered outcrops, the wide arms of western bays, waiting to birth their blood-streaked pups, nursing and nuzzling them into the salty waves.

Amidst near islands, last year's brood dive and fish in unbroken abandon.

In distant seas the great grey bull turns towards Seal Rock.

And I am pulled back. The time is coming, if only I can remain, waiting.

'Morning, how's things today?'

'Fine thanks.'

Brown on fair skin. High cheekbones.

'Bit fresh last night was it not? Are you able to sleep in that wee tent?'

See the green eyes.

'It's ok, quite comfortable.'

Still wrapped up in an anorak and two rugs. Hair pulled back tight under a beanie.

'The wind would keep me awake. I don't like that noise when it sucks the canvas back out – vrrump. Then you lie there waiting. You know it'll whump back in any moment.'

'How do you know that?'

'I lived in tents for a while with my work.'

'If the wind wakes me up, I go out to see what's happening on my shoreline.'

'Your shore?'

First hint of a smile. I might not be Count Dracula.

'Well, I seem to be looking after it for now anyway.'

'Fair enough. What happens but if a really big gale gets up?'

'I can retreat into the cave there. It's completely sheltered.'

'How come?'

'It twists round into the bank. Look, I need to be getting on.'

'I saw you writing as I came down.'

'Just my workplan for each day.'

'Do you not record your observations?'

'Sometimes.'

'Things round here seem to shift from minute to minute.'

She looks as if seeing me for the first time, then turns back to her daily task.

'Right then, I'll maybe come around later.'

Off along the sandy beach to see what the tide's brought in. Routine, discipline is what this boy requires. Finding an order between these tides. Is that what she's after with the art thing? Jesus, forgot to introduce myself. Don't even know her name, numptie. Not even half your father's son.

Might see a bit of sun today though. Stretch out the old pins. Listen to those waves gurgling in, lapping out. Those waders know their business, howking out breakfast beneath screeching gulls. Go on man, get some of that air into your lungs and blow it back out through the wind.

Maybe we could try some breakfast ourselves.

A struggle to get going this morning. Woke at three o'clock with wind whipping the canvas, and cold. Forced myself out and was rewarded by real waves breaking. The sound of course, but also the strange whiteness of foam catching the light of a crescent moon between clouds. Weird cries on the wind like signals of distress. Maybe seals disturbed by the big sea on their rocks. It must be much rougher on the point.

What I need is a studio, to go and paint without interruption, laying on blacks and blues as the bed for all those gleams, glimmers, glints. Instead, I was driven back into the tent, unable to get warm. Shivering with the cries. Slipped eventually into sleep and woke late. Morning calmer, but still cool.

Jobs for today:

Check my tide wall for damage – is it being reclaimed?

Walk along the beach to sift the debris – spindrift from last night's wind. Any new seaweeds, mix of dulse and tangle. The birds seem to be at the same sorting out, but I can't tell one species from another.

Interrupted next by the man from yesterday. Irish, Northern Irish by his accent. He must be the new holiday let in the croft house, but the first one to take any interest in me. Polite or over interested – in art? Looks a bit worn, as if he has been ill. Eventually he totters off along the beach leaving me alone. The beach is visible from the croft but not my tent or cave.

Change of tack. The island is in clear focus this morning – grassy humps edged with rock like a bald head fringed with hair. Waves breaking white. Do a series of sketches tracing that oscillating image, yet somehow rock constant, always re-emergent, resurgent.

Eilean na Cleirich, says Mr MacLean, Island of the Priests. Can it ever have sustained life? Seabirds yes but tonsured monks? Only in extreme fast or penance. Maybe they were artists of their age. Clarity of eye, austerity of soul, and in their stone cells they lit a fire to preserve some spark of warmth. Redder than calor gas can offer. Still, it is a germ of heat.

Time to brew a restoring cup and set to work.

This is a day with summer still in it. The tourists can be having a fine view out to Islay and Jura, and to Ireland if they go high enough on this ridge. They love their views, like picture post-cards. But they see nothing.

Even our young visitor from Ireland is on the beach today. He does not look well. I am thinking he might have cancer and has come here to recover from the chemotherapy. Pumping the poison through his body, kill or cure.

The marker cairns have crumbled so you would hardly know they had ever been. Coffins carried along to the burial ground and at each resting place another stone. Cairns of memory, for the old people. The only one remaining is where the path meets the new road up for cars. Funerals come yet, and that foolish young minister from Glasgow with his keelie ways – outdoor services and picnics in this of all places. Clambering over the stones without knowledge or respect.

There was a whole village here, clustered round the church. The traces of each house remain, and the big hearths at the centre. Till the killing and burning came on them. No-one remembers now. Though I remember.

A storyteller without listeners is not worthy of the name.

The cross they make so much of shelters in the chapel, so that it will not erode further. They are mistaken in naming it Abba's Cross, for it was raised by the sons of Artur Mac Aedan, a prince of Dalriada. He was slain fighting the Picts, but later his descendants settled here around the church. Abba was earlier, before the high cross was raised. Yet he was not the first to use the headland. He came from Ireland seeking the place of his resurrection and did not find it here. There was some trouble between his community and the house of the women by the rock well. So the tradition has it, and he took voyage to the north, the ends of the earth.

Perhaps he had a gift of prophecy, for there were only a few years left before the sea wolves nosed their longships onto the beach. The folk fled at first sight, but not the cowled ones. The raiders scattered out from their landfall loping up onto this ridge and heading towards the enclosure. The monks gathered in their chapel like lambs dressed for the slaughter. And the altar ran crimson from their wounds, the blood of Christ. They had gained their prize, the red martyrdom.

Without a second glance those savage men bundled the sacred treasures, chalice, patten, candlesticks, into their sacks and hurried back to the ships. They met no resistance for none was prepared for such merciless assault, the unexpected fury as if from the depths of hell itself, so swift and deadly and cruel.

That was the beginning of the killing times, always a price to be paid, a sacrifice offered or taken by violence. The pattern of this place, endless giving and taking, land and sea. Yet the Women's House endured, their tradition long lived.

Our artist, Ms Lucy as I must learn to call her, seemed most interested in that, and in Abba's Island in the bay. Perhaps she herself has come in search of sanctuary.

Only the most recent graves are tended here now. The memory of those times buried as if they never were, as if sunk in Brigid's unfathomable mind. Perhaps such forgetting is for the best, who knows?

I think I shall not go as far as the headland today. I can see the sun on the stones, and that is enough.

Sat myself down and went out like a light. Put it down to sea and sun. Or wind. All the way to the landing place, up to the village and back along the ridge. Alpine circuit.

Came to early afternoon and straight outside again. A few puffy clouds drifting over light-blue sky and deep-blue sea. The tourist crowd have it made on this spot. Like those islands are sailing off to the end of the world, but serenely. Needs our artist woman to deal with that, not a hacked-out observer like your man here. She should come up to get an eyeful.

Then suddenly old MacLean's alongside me again. Out of the blue you might say – how does he manage it? There must be five, six miles between the village and the headland but nothing moves without his notice. A hawk squaring its ground. There was a big bird up high today as well, maybe an eagle.

'How are you today, Mr MacArthur?'

'Very well, thank you. It's a fine day.'

'A fine day indeed, and it may hold for a few days to come.'

'That would be grand. How far is it along to the church? I hear it's worth a visit.'

'Why would that be?'

'Well for its history I suppose. And the high cross is quite famous, is it not?'

'Indeed, that is so.' He was studying me intently. 'You will not be knowing that your own family name is connected to the chapel?'

'No, no idea – nothing about it in the guidebook.'

'The guidebooks are written by the English. MacArthurs lived in a village around the chapel; and were buried there.'

'When was that?'

'Many generations past. Did your own people come from Scotland?'

'Not that I know, my father was from Donegal.'

'Yes, indeed, Donegal. They were often going from here to Donegal. With a fair wind you can be off Inishowen in less than five hours under sail.'

'I'm no sailor, couldn't even row. I'd like to read up on that history though.'

'There are few books that tell these things. I will be wishing you a good day.'

He's off before I can ask him about the eagle. With that loping stride of his, white hair and beard aloft.

Still, I'm intrigued – some family connection with the ragtag McArthurs of Donegal, sheep farmers and muckers to a man. I could be descended from a clan chief fallen on hard times, back here now on my ancestral turf. Go into the house with a wee sense of ownership. Will need to winkle out some more information from His MacLeanship, the current guardian.

Time for a proper spot of cooking. First since arriving. Slice up an onion and into the foot of the pan. Touch of garlic next, chicken pieces I bought this morning, and then a tin of tomatoes. Opened a bottle of wine and sloshed in a pourful or two. Filled myself a celebration glass.

Celebrating what? Well, that's the point. Feeling half human today.

Work has piled up on the dresser out there in the lobby. Let it be. Switch on the radio and wait for chicken to mellow. Chill. After all, I have earned it; the boy's made it home, come good at the end. No point leaving an open bottle to sour.

'Four more through the night, and two more as the sun came up. That's nine altogether so far, but the mothers are still coming in, heaving up the rock, poor souls. It looks like a bumper year. Their menfolk have all swum off, as you would expect, but for one or two youngsters who have no idea what to do with themselves.

'No time at all though and the first pups will be in the water, but for now suck, suck and gurgle, all the lovely sounds.

'The young woman is still there on the beach, Bridie. She seems to have no interest in the seals. Strange, I thought at first that was why she had come – for the birthing season, a wee bit ahead of herself. She spends her time staring at the sea and shore, writing in a book, or drawing on big pads. An artist, but then she shuffles stones and driftwood on the beach like a child, intent only on what she is doing, on what she notices in her own mind. Surely, she must be hearing the seals?

'Thank you, I will have a cup of tea. And you're right, Bridie, of course. Time is early for her. Who knows what she may see and feel, especially at this season. Aye, and I must be going out soon to watch for the new arrivals. We don't want the men going to the point. You know what I mean, of course you do, dear, but don't fret, Bridie, it will be alright. We will watch over the people of the sea, you and I, like sisters. There now, I've kissed you on the brow, for we can still give one another the peace.'

A day's work almost frustrated. Warm and sunny with a few cirrhus clouds drifting across the sky. Every island from Eilean na Cleirich out to Islay and Jura vivid yet unsubstantial, surreal – like recessive hallucinations. Impossible, much too much.

I turned my back and studied the cliff, more like a steep bank, that defines the beaches, separating rock and sand from the grassier uplands. The stone is hard, dark-grey limestone with the striations at points almost vertical. There is supposed to be a basalt outcrop somewhere, signing the volcanic forces that shaped this rockscape. But now it is home to grasses, sedges and flowers – campions, sea pansies and spurrey cling to its cracks and fissures. The ramparts hold out against the weather.

That is why these steps are no trick of nature but a human intervention, taking advantage of the fault line from which my cave derives its existence. There too some human hand has cut into the rock to accentuate the twist that gives the inner space depth and shelter.

I move straight from the drawings to two big paintings. Taking advantage of the dry, clear light but turning away from the myriad sparkle of sea. Layer that stony face with its decorative tufts and little spurts of red and pink. As if that was the studio wall and I was looking at my subject in a mirror.

So, in the end satisfaction, and I lay them out to dry in a breeze that barely lifts the paper's edge. Constructive work carried through to its endpoint. Grant myself a bottle of beer from the cave's dim recesses.

Watching the sun go down – pinks, orange, blood red, deep crimson, dark. No more. To bed and musky warmth. Sleep the sleep of the spent, sunk in unremembered dreams.

Come awake abruptly. Radio still grizzling. Plate, glass and bottle around my feet. Dark but not wholly dark. There were cries in my sleep, moans of pain. Again.

Up and out to bathe in the cool air.

Above a sheen of sky, pinpricked by a million shining dots of light. But cries and barks carried from the sea
beneath a sliver of cold moon. Distant, yet strangely close.
That's those seals at the point, no dream. Haunting all the
same, though – some passage, agony of the night. Must be
the mating season.

I was back beside the tents, beneath the perfect dome
of stars. The seal calls pull me to this place. The night's soft
around my head, thank God. I go to bed and lie awake, letting
my thoughts come unbidden, without fear or question.

Sketching with the first rays of sun on the beach. Herring gulls
and blackbacks wheeling to catch the light. Learning to name
their kinds. The sand glints and sparkles and even my tumbledown dyke seems to absorb some lustre.

Time to pause, make some tea, boiled eggs and toast. All
that unbroken sleep makes you hungry. I seem to be settling in,
finding my rhythm at last.

I can make this work. If I shut out everything else.

Should plan my day but the island is coming alive, as the
sun rises picking out its knolls and little hollows. I wonder if
Mr MacLean would drop me off there for a day to explore. Perhaps I could stay a night, like St Abba, if the weather was fine.

'Morning. Anyone at home?'

'Sorry, I was watching the island.'

'Lovely isn't it. We might be in for another good day.'

'Hope so.'

He was following my gaze out into the bay. Narrow face, a bit gaunt, with short grey hair brushed back. Something wary, but when he looks round the eyes are warm, noticing.

'How long are you going to work here?'

'I'm planning on six weeks, just over halfway. It should lead to an exhibition next year if I can get the work done.'

'I'm Dave, Dave McArthur.'

'Lucy, Salter. I'm not famous or anything.'

'Not yet. I'm long-term unfamous.'

'Are you staying at the Well Croft?'

'Aye, up above the beach here. Amazing views out to sea when it's clear. You should come up and paint it.'

'Too much to take in, for now anyway. We'll see how it goes. Are you on holiday or working?'

'Bit of report writing officially, but mainly holiday.'

About to say something more but then changed his mind.

'Have you found your well yet?'

'Sorry?'

'At the cottage.'

'Right, no. Is there still a well?'

'Out in the back yard beneath a big stone slab. Mr MacLean showed me.'

'He knows everything round here.'

'Apparently there was a community of religious there, all women. The croft was built on the site, probably with the same stone and foundations.'

'It's old enough anyway. MacLean was telling me about the church too, chapel as he calls it.'

'They were separate – the monastery and the Women's House – but connected in some way originally.'

'That makes me a kind of trespasser then. But I like it up there, sort of peaceful.'

'When the women wanted to be really alone, they came down here to my cave.'

'A solitude trip. You're set up then in your own wee hermitage.'

'Very comfortable too; there's a freshwater spring inside the cave mouth.'

'Sea for baths.'

'I can go to Mr MacLean's when I need a shower. He's been very kind.'

'A kind of guardian spirit. He seems to have lived here forever.'

'That's a rare thing nowadays.'

'Something seems to rub off on you though, even after a few days. As if you've been here forever too.'

'I know what you mean. I feel that as well. Maybe it's the sea, drawing you into its patterns. I have to plan everything round the tides.'

'An artist prepares. Well, I'm off to the shop. Can I get you anything?'

'Not today, thanks.'

'I'll leave you to your solitude.'

'You're kidding. There's always something happening on the beach. Why don't you look down sometime and see my work?'

'I might take you up on that. Seeing in a new way, and so on.'

Off with a friendly half wave, taking his line along the high-water mark, occasional pause to look seawards. Seems a nice guy, though he's not telling why he came here.

Right, food and that workplan.

She is very restless today. When I moved her from the bedroom as is usual, she struggled to leave, remembering the back door and the way out onto the hill. Then she went back to her seat, twisting and turning with a low moan or whimper, refusing to settle.

I have not seen her like this before, turning away from the fire to face something that is troubling her outside. But things are no different from normal at this time of year. Unless it might be the seals she is hearing.

I shall be going up for the nurse, to ask for her to visit. She likes the new nurse because she has some words of Gaelic. Brigid has lost nearly all her words, but most of all the English.

This road from the landing place is part of the village now with tarmac pavements. There are bungalows on both sides, where the infields used to come down to meet the track. You could collect a boat's crew from the crofts on either side, but nowadays the fishermen come from all over. The whole village has only two for a lifeboat crew. Soon there may be none. Yet the place is bustling with visitors. The harbour is pretty with little boats and pleasure craft – good business even for the landing place. If I was younger, would we be opening a cafe?

There is no sign of the nurse's car. I will be needing to wait.

'Hush now, my dear, *mo cridhe*. All is well. They are coming in without harm. The people of the sea still have their protector. Make the sign with me, Bridie.

'That's better.

'We'll take our tea; it's a good cup, warm in the hands. Just grand. I'm pleased you like the new Nurse. It's a blessing to have Gaelic in the house.

'Shall we tell the story, Bride? Abba of the seals, when he was born. You like a story, especially one we've heard before. It's a comfort for anxious days.

'Where shall I start... when Abba was born, a little baby in the desert cave. And it was hard because she was alone and afraid. But there was a freshwater spring in the mouth of the cave; it kept mother and baby alive and she was able to wash their bodies after the birth. She had not noticed that spring when she arrived, exhausted and in pain.

'Yes, maybe she was not alone? You think she felt some kind of presence there.

'But what was I to do with the child, the little boy. I could not go back to the village where they would expose my baby to die, or give him to the peasants for a slave. I knew that the monks' cells were not far away, clustered like beehives below the edge of the wadi. So taking my basket, I laid little Abba in the foot, cradled in his swaddling bands.

'After darkness had washed over the desert, I went out beneath the cold stars. Ignoring the cries of wild beasts, I stole to the wadi and placed my basket at the door of the nearest cell. Then I went back to the edge behind a rock and huddling in my wrap, waited to see what would happen.

'Just before dawn the holy Father came out of his cell, an old bent man. He stared at the basket, then lifted it in his arms and carried it back inside. Then I knew that all would be well for the little one.

'My prayers had been heard, Bridie, but the mother could not then foresee how her life and his would remain entwined.'

Farseeing mercy; stories for another day.

She is sleeping now like a baby, at peace, whatever dreams may come to haunt her rest. There are voices at her door. Nurse will be wondering what himself is fussing about, like a broody old mother hen.

They come through a grey dawn. Over the slippery rocks, where bloody smears of afterbirth wait to be scavenged by the tide.

Soft, fatty pups wriggle amongst the milky cows who nuzzle and shift and shove as new seals clamber out of a sullen sea into the fluid mass.

Landlocked. Vulnerable, trusting in survival.

The boats slide in and slithering in their oilskins men clamber onto the rocks.

And the clubs swing again and again, bruising, crunching, cracking. Blood and mucus in the foam. Flesh compacted; fibrous flippers broken.

Lust to kill fed by thrashing bodies, moans heaved from chest and throat. The squeals of severed pups. Brains spill from split skulls like human seed.

Easy on the lunch; I'm on an outing today, to the McArthur sanctuary. Cheese, brown bread and a glass of milk. Couldn't face the apple.

According to the map it's a bit over a mile to the church. Feels longer on the ground. The route's direct though along the ridge at the back of Well Croft. You can almost step right onto it out of my wee causie. Still to find the well.

No sighting of Donald MacLean today though this is his beat, as far as the church or right out to the point. The path seems well worn, yet he's the only walker I've seen on it so far. Excepting myself, mind you. Might be busier in the main season. Maybe the sheep wear it down as there's always a smattering of them, though not going anywhere as far as I can tell.

Eyes right at first onto the bay, as another low rise blocks the view east. More sheep that way, tussocky grass and rock. Whatever brought folk here wasn't the soil. More sea and shelter, coming up the channel to Jura, into the loch and its harbour, or maybe MacLean's landing place further up the peninsula, on the sea side.

It's all in plain view from up here, anyroads. The bay's too small to get a boat of any size, too shallow, rocky on both sides and the island narrows the access anyway – depending on the tide. Once in though you're well protected. It's a perfect sanctuary, unless your attackers know the ground well. Maybe that's what brings the seals here, so close to shore.

Looks like the island was once part of the coastline, running evenly up to the landing place. Gradually broken down by the sea, those strong currents in the strait. Turning into a right wee survey now. The training kicks in – geology, landform, climate, then the settlement patterns. Somewhere in there you find the start of the troubles. Need to know the lie of the land. History's lies. All those reports unread, lessons unlearned.

Which is why you're along here, instead of staring at the stockpile back in the lobby.

Look back now and you can see the bay from the south side – just the sand and the low arm. No sign of Lucy, but then she's tucked in below the bluff, dead centre of the arc. Hidden from here, and so steep you need steps to get down.

Still, you think she might be out doing her arty scavenging – found objects, as they say. For every person who makes or does something there's at least four to theorise and write reports on it. She's trying to get close up to the thing itself. Bone beneath the skin. Seems a nice woman to turn herself into a hermit.

Into the fringe of a wood the path goes next. Conifers mainly, stretching down towards the loch. Seems to peter out on this side with a few stunted birches and a scatter of gorse. So much for sea air. 'You'll see the deer along there,' according to the chief guide, but all that's moving today are gulls and a few sheep. No, tell a lie, there are some crows as well, or ravens.

In five minutes I'm clear of the trees, such as they are, but coming out you've dropped down below the ridge, on the inland side. There's the sea loch now below, long and narrow, and the other shore completely wooded. And behind that, a good way back, some big hills. Very peaceful down there, still and shiny, with a couple of yachts and other wee boats chugging in and out, windless. Bonny Scotland right enough. The guidebooks don't lie. Unless about the weather.

The path goes along the top of a lower ridge that slopes down to boggy fields beside the loch. Grass is greener on this side though, broken up with rushes and gorse rather than rock. Cultivated ground maybe at one time, fed by seaweed and manure from the cows that are still trailing about down in the bog.

Big, rough wall visible now, and the church roof sticking up above it. But before you get there you're walking through low tumbled ruins, just clusters of stone in some places. Here, and higher up, houses once spilling down the slope. Five, six, seven, eight, more probably. Other outhouses, walls enclosing a real settlement – lost, abandoned. Attached to the church once, overseeing the loch? No-one to tell us now, apart from Donald MacLean.

The church wall is a later build, protecting a much smaller site. Keeping sheep and deer out of the graveyard. The grass has been cut, daisies and roses here and there among a big spread of gravestones, some quite recent. Campbells, MacDonalds, MacLeans, no sign of those fabled MacArthurs.

The church seems a plain rectangular block, raised up a bit higher on some rock, so you see further south right down to the headland. Featureless till you reach the point where some strange rock formations huddle like shawled wifies on a pier. Standing stones maybe, after centuries of weather. Touch of breeze up here, nice after the walking.

Lift the latch, door opens, and step in.

Empty. Quiet. A few benches in rows on the flagged floor. Facing the big stone cross at the far end. Sunlight from the gable behind.

It really is massive, intricately carved beneath the weathering. Beasts, monks, ships, angels, demons – dream signs from a lost world. Impressive, but shut up here at a land's end. No-one to read or understand the messages.

Surprisingly cold in here. The walls must be thick despite the external plainness. Shadows and casts of light. Two interpretation boards to the side, and bronze plaques where I came in. Three panels like a war memorial. Just a few names on each, but all MacArthur – Macs not Mics. Lt-Colonel this and Brigadier that... due to the long association with this place, and their family's service to the Argyll and Sutherland Highlanders, and so forth.

So, are they buried here, or just staking some kind of claim? Nineteenth and twentieth-century dates, fronting the Empire, keeping down the peasants and repulsing other would-be colonisers. Upper class MacArthurs, not Donegal farmers. MacLean was right though.

Have I seen enough?

It comes at me. From somewhere behind the cross, fast-moving shadow, tight at the throat, choking grip. I'm tearing at the band with both hands, gives without warning. I break free out the door, starting to run, straight for the wall, scrambling, scraping for handholds.

Over through the tangle of stones, and onto the path rasping for breath.

Glancing back. There's nothing behind me. No-one.

Drawing air, I can see in every direction. Deserted. What was in that church? Intruder, phantom of a tired mind, devil? I'm not going back to find out. Once is enough.

Slowing, calmer beat.

Was that flash a weapon? Knife, machete even? Why was the figure so dark – maybe wearing something light. A headdress. Darfur back in my contorted brain? Please not. Some escaped madman lurking here? Aye, like me.

Need to get back home and patch these grazes. Feels like skint knees as well. No headland for you. Prescribed regime, strictly domestic. And some sweeties.

She is rarely settled so early. I can go down to see the boats put out into the western sun. There is a change in the air though. The wind is turning from the further sea and quickening. Grey clouds will be coming in through the darkness to cloak us in rain tomorrow. This fine week could not be lasting.

Perhaps it is the changing weather that was upsetting her. Yet there is hardly enough in it to be disturbing herself. Sometimes she is like one of the waking dead and all the years there have been between us turn to dust in her unseeing eye.

There is still light in the sky and promise for a spread of stars. I will go along the rise after and check on Ms Lucy. The seals are restless with their birthing and who is to say a seal might not come up to the cave for shelter and frighten her with its cries and smell.

If any comes near her, I can kill it – on that pretext. Since the cull was proscribed they have become too many on this coast. If Abba had been harder on these sea cows when they came ashore, then the lamp oil may have yet burned brightly in his chapel. There is no help for weakness.

The beach is quiet tonight except for lapping of the waves. I did not warn her that sometimes the submarines rise up amongst the islands, and their crew send out a dinghy on exercise. These vessels snag nets and could drag the fishermen under. But they will not be owning up to such a thing. They have power to destroy the earth at one press of a button. Passing to-and-fro silent and deadly, harnessing the secret power of nature in defiance of His laws.

Sometimes I think that God has left us here to our solitary ends. The church pews are empty and the Sabbath desecrated.

She must be safely in her tent, the artist, waiting for another dawn to scribble these disordered pictures she calls her sketches. What is it that Ms Lucy seeks here? What dream or vision of herself? Yet she is a hardy woman outstaying all weathers. The old people would be acknowledging that in her praise. There have been hardy women in this place for many generations. My own Brigid was of their lineage.

I will return by Well Croft, keeping to the ridge, pacing out these hours of summer night before the rain. It is good to be walking under the stars.

There is a light yet at the croft window. Is MacArthur not sleeping? A dark shadow is at the gable. Himself, pissing into the night, as if he had no urinal indoors.

Well, many a one has pissed there before him, with more cause. He is turning back into the lobby, swaying and unsteady. He has the drink on him without doubt, the drink of despair or discontent, no abandon of the spirits. There is something troubling that Irishman and I hope his troubles will not break our peace. Tomorrow I shall be calling at the Well House.

The great grey ships are gathering over Jura. God will piss on us all tonight.

Rasp for breath, charred in the nostrils, acrid mouth.

Burning, more choking bodies. Fires. Let this rain damp the fires.

Everything is black, smoke watering our eyes till there is more night than day.

Stumbling over debris, broken earthenware, scattered tools. Wooden stakes still mark each circle where huts stood. One more abandoned village.

Another community burnt out from their homes, shot, sworded, trampled down. And worse. Helpless before death's riders.

Now rain is running down my face. Clouds big with mercy.

Everything is wrapped in damp grey wet. Muffling and obscuring. Visibility minimal, with even our island only appearing now and then through variable patches.

My sleeping bag, blankets, clothes and shoes are all damp. At least it's warm wet.

Work on paper is out today, so I plan another construction, built with pebbles and wet sand in the intertidal gap, below the remains of my wall. A kind of sandcastle formed from the only materials readily available, firmly compacted but transitory. Temporary engineering, like a beavers' dam. Like all human construction in a more distant lens.

I will photograph the building and then record its dissolution. I can create a network of watercourses around the construction to delay its disintegration, but I expect it will be undermined first, sapped by the back draw of outgoing tides.

If I keep focussed this will take me through the weather, since it looks like the beach will be closed in all day. That has its own attractions – I can move undisturbed within the veil.

Pounding head, nursing a warm cup between my paws, when the knock came.

MacLean. I asked him in, and he took the proffered tea.

'Terrible day.'

'It may rain for a few days.'

'Really?'

'It has been known.'

'Aye.'

'I am hoping you are staying well, Mr MacArthur.'

'Not quite top of the range today, Mr....Listen, I'm Dave, could you call me Dave?'

'Of course. My name is Donald, Donald MacLean.'

'Yes, well, Donald, truth be told, there was some drink taken last night.'

'I am sorry to hear that – Dave.'

'Don't be, it was fine at the time. Not so great this morning.'

'That is the way of it. What took you to drinking, Dave?'

'Hard to say exactly. But I did have a strange experience at the church yesterday. I thought there...'

'You were at St Abba's sanctuary, in the chapel?'

'Yes, I thought I should pay my respects, so I had a nosy round and went into the chapel.'

'To see the cross.'

'Right. It felt very chill in there, and dim. And someone, something – came at me.'

'You were attacked?'

'Not sure. I may have imagined it, but I felt as if someone tried to grab me from behind, by the throat. There was a knife, or some weapon, and I had to break free. I ran out and over the wall.'

'You escaped.'

'Something in there did not like me, or something in me.'

'Are you having dreams, Dave?'

'Well, that's it. I've been working in the Sudan, in Darfur, as a peacekeeper, would-be peacekeeper, and my mind's full of it.'

'Darfur is a place of trouble. I am sorry for the poor people there. What kind of peacekeeper were you?'

'Not much of one. Just trying to record the breaches and atrocities. Some form of testimony. There were terrible things.... seen... done...'

'There, now, Dave, don't take it on yourself. Here's a drop of whisky to your tea.'

The silver flask came out and then was deftly tucked away.

'Tail of the dog. Thanks.'

'Many years ago, I was myself in Aden.'

'During the war?'

'Insurgency, they called it at that time.'

'You were in the army.'

'The Argyll and Sutherlands. It was a dirty war, and sometimes the pictures still return to my own mind. It is good to be out on the hill when that happens and the shore, where such memories may be dispersed in the face of the day. Now, if you are rested, I must be on my way. I will be about the place if you are needing me at any time.'

'Right. I appreciate that, Donald. Just before you go though, could you show me where the well is?'

'You know of the well?'

'Lucy mentioned it to me.'

'Ah, Ms Lucy. Indeed, it is not a hard thing to find.'

I got up, still a mite shooglie, and followed him out into the causie. Rain still steady. He went to a large flagstone near the village end and raised it with an easy movement onto its edge. I peered down beside him into a receding stone-lined shaft – beautifully worked. A dark, mossy odour, no glint of the bottom.

'The water is pure and sweet to this day.'

He lowered the flag gently into position, re-covering the well, with a small out breath of satisfaction.

'How long has it been there?'

'As long as this place has been here. Since the time of Abba or perhaps before.'

'It's the real deal. Thanks for showing me, Donald. It's good somehow to think that it exists there beneath us, even if you can't see it.'

'Indeed.'

He turned as if to head off along the path, and then seemed to hesitate, half swinging back.

'Once in the chapel, David, there was a terrible thing that happened.'

'Inside the church?'

'The people were driven in there, the door barred and fire put to the thatch. Some broke out to be killed but most smothered in the smoke.'

'Were many killed? Why were they massacred?'

'I shall tell you the whole story one day.'

'Maybe the spirit of that time came after me.'

If this was humour, it was ignored.

'That could be. Maybe you opened yourself to attack. For now, you had better be going in from the rain.'

This time he was off, loping into the mist.

I stood shivering in the yard, as if the backdraught of some centuries old trouble had caught me here. Glad of the well beneath. I shook myself and hurried into the fire. At least home was not a tent.

'What is it, Bridie?'

Emitting low moans, turning to-and-fro. But not distressed.

'You want that story. When Abba was by himself on Eilean na Cleirich. You remember, the healing of the bull. He was in the cell there, eating little and sleeping less, living by prayer, with some bread and water.'

And she settles to the rhythm, something familiar and once understood.

'The island was his desert place, as the cave provided for the Well House. One night Abba was woken by eerie cries and groans. A young bull had dragged himself up onto a rocky ledge, thrashing in pain. By the light of a crescent moon, Abba could see the cause of his distress. A hunter's blade was thrust into the creature's side up to the hilt. What painful effort it had cost the bull to drag himself out of the water.'

She moans in sympathy, sounding the pain.

'But now his strength was ebbing, his groans subsiding. Without some relief he would die there on the exposed shelf. Abba stepped onto the ledge and sidestepping the thrash of muscle, he soothed the beast with words of blessing. Then with gentle touch, inch by inch, he drew out the knife. Next, running to his herb patch he pulled fresh leaves and laid them in the wound, easing the puckered edges softly together, closing the gash against raw air and infection.

'From fear and exhausted rage the great seal subsided, submitting to Abba's ministrations. On three successive days the herbal dressing was refreshed. Finally, on the third day, the bull slid back into the water, and after long gaze into the healer's eyes, he swam off with easy strength into the strait and open sea beyond.

'In following days, the seals came to visit Abba bringing fish in their mouths and frolicking round his refuge. But he did not see the bull again.'

She is trying to tell me something, I am sure of it. There is another part to this story.

'Aye, Bridie, like Abba you understand their language, the help given to their kind. The help they can give back, pray God. May He grant you rest and better sleep.'

The construction was a success. Moat channelling the sea, banks, towers, walls studded with shells and pebbles.

Memories come back of building sandcastles as a child, or at least helping my father make them. He was enthusiastic about that, a beach dad in his element. Time suspended.

But suddenly the tide was sweeping back in, and I realised how cold I was, soaked through. I forced myself to get the camera. Rain was running down the lens, as well as my face, as if the image was being washed away along with the compacted sand.

So, I just stood and watched the work disintegrate, dissolve, as the water in my eyes and on my cheeks merged with salt waves.

I needed warmth, and instead of huddling back into the tent, I began to run along the beach. By the time I reached the landing place I had stopped shaking, and pressed Mr. MacLean's bell. He seemed unfazed by my breathless arrival and ushered me through to the bathroom, encouraging me to use everything I needed in the way of hot water and towels – 'not a day to be letting the chill take hold'.

I filled the big bath to its brim and sank gratefully into the steaming heat, emptying my mind, surrendering my body.

As I gradually came round I washed, dried myself with a generous allowance of towel and donned a lime green dressing gown from the back of the bathroom door, presumably the invalid Mrs MacLean's. I spread my own clothes over the towel rail to dry.

By the time I came through to the sitting-room, there was a coal fire alight in the grate, and my host was laying out teacups and shortbread.

'Sit by the fire now, it's a terrible wet day.'

'I'm much warmer thanks – the bath was a life saver.'

I took the cup of tea which he poured and sipped thankfully. There was no sign of Mrs MacLean; she seemed to exist somewhere in the back of the cottage.

'You could not be painting in this rain.'

'I was building sandcastles and then trying to photograph them.'

'I see.'

I laughed, but nevertheless tried to explain.

'It's a kind of instant art, here today and gone tomorrow.'

'I would not myself be thinking of that as art.'

'It's just the idea, the concept.'

'Indeed. Would you like to phone your family?'

'I'm fine, thank you. I can use the phone box in the village. I didn't realise my mobile would be useless here.'

'You are welcome to use the phone here whenever you need. Your family will be worrying.'

'The mad artist. My partner Ian is very supportive of what I am doing.'

'That is good. It's strange for me to think of, as we could not be doing such a thing when we were younger.'

'Have you been married a long time?'

'More than fifty years. But Brigid does not keep well. She is lost in her mind.'

'I'm sorry, that must be difficult.'

'Dementia they call it.'

'Perhaps I could look in and visit, chat with her?'

'She has no conversation. We must accept what is allowed to us.'

'I suppose so.'

'Is the Irishman disturbing you?'

'No. He comes to the beach now and then for a chat. He seems very nice.'

'Indeed. I am not sure he is completely well in himself.'

'Bit strained perhaps.'

'If he behaves strangely at all –'

'Don't worry, Mr MacLean, I'll be able to look after myself.'

'Of course, but I would not have your family worrying.'

'That's very kind of you. I'll go and see if my things are dry. And many thanks for the tea. You've saved my life today.'

I pulled on my still damp clothes and walked back to the beach through slackening rain. I moved the stove and bedding from the tent into the cave and set up to spend my first night there since arriving.

Now whatever comes, I'll be ready for another day.

Darfur is a more complicated situation than people realise. It goes way back, but the start of the modern business was down to the English, or even God help us the Irish. James Vandeleur Kelly, of landlord fame, led a conquering army into the ancient African Kingdom of Darfur in 1916. When, you may recall, we were fighting World War I alongside our allies the French. Nonetheless, the boyos in London thought the French, the allied ones, might muscle in from Chad to the west. So they send in the mighty Vandeleur with a wee expedition which hadn't yet been slaughtered on the Somme, like half the sons of Ulster – McArthurs of Donegal included.

Now we've annexed it what do we do? Well, nothing. Just let the inhabitants get on with normal business, agricultural mostly, besides some traditional self-government. Goats and cows to the south, and Arab camel herders in the north. The ancient trade routes have mainly died out. They're all Muslim nowadays, regardless of race.

Time rolls on. Then in the fifties, nineteen-fifties, Egypt and Sudan get independence while the Brits get a bloody nose. The new regime is Arab, based in Sudan's Nile heartland, so they impose direct rule on Darfur. It's Ireland all over again. Local officials are dismissed, and the new colonials arrive from Khartoum to take control.

That starts stirrings of resistance, but it takes coups in Sudan and Egypt, and drought in the eighties to really set the tinder alight. Too many people for too little water. The locals rise against Khartoum, and the reaction is brutal, fascist. Land-grabbing, clearance, ethnic cleansing, genocide.

And the willing tools are those northern herders. They form mobile killing units, Janjaweed militia on camels, aided and abetted by the Sudanese airforce. It's become an Arab crusade. The idea was to grind away in remote sub-Sahara, when all eyes were on civil war in South Sudan. Then that stuttered to a close, so they stepped up the pace in Darfur, and the world began to notice – not to stop it but to notice. Recording events, for wider consideration.

What consideration? To name the killing for the war crime it is. And the underlying lesson – to show that violence still pays because those ruthless enough to apply shocking and systematic force can succeed in our new world order, same as the old. But the real consequence is what comes next. How many more regimes will go down this road, how many more massacres will be applied because we failed to stop this one, or even to penalise the perpetrators?

Why are these deadly patterns so easy to fall into? Because they run in well-worn grooves. Time out of mind; peacekeepers are the deluded. So, what's the point of another bloody report?

Following some underwater signal, synchronised, they come in. Two, then three, then five, or nine, till the rocks are awash with slubberie bodies.

A chorus of grunts and moans echoes through inner passages, issuing eerily into the moist mass of muffled dark.

She steps amongst them as a shadow, touching, coaxing, pushing, as one after another the slimy pups surge through the mouths of flesh, slide, swim into their unknown elements of air and sea.

Under its grey veil, Seal Point moves like an undulating sea. Necks and bodies turn to gnaw cords free, lick, clean, stroke the freshly birthed.

She loses count of the new arrivals as lessening dark merges into lightening dawn. One labouring cow remains exhausted, unrelieved, crying to the light that will not break through. Bending close, the hands massage and press and stretch until she reaches in and pulls on every hold her hand can manage. The pressure gives, and out the baby comes.

Too late. Inert, immobile on the rock. No response to sniff, lick, nudge. She gathers up the bloody little corpse and casts it back into the cleansing sea.

The mother barks her pain but lives to bear another season.

TWO

TODAY'S ANOTHER IN the pattern. Four days. The morning is bright with just a few scattered clouds, but there is something in the air – clearer than bright. Like crystal dissolved into liquid. Then in early afternoon a wind picks up and showers roll in from the straits. By teatime they have blown over leaving a soft evening glow. Then comes the climax – golden horizon and a blazing, fiery sunset behind the islands.

Constructions abandoned, worked without stopping, sketch in crayon, paint, attempting to follow that sequence, pursue each atmospheric shift. Moment by moment transmutations, impossible, merging of flows of light and colour, as if the land itself was being perpetually remixed.

Bewildering, but cumulatively I am soothed, surrendering hand and eye. Always behindhand, yet somehow keeping in step. Somewhere in the work that pattern will re-emerge. I am beginning to rely on that, a self beyond my so-called powers of observation – that narrow I.

Dave comes round each day. I expect his late afternoon visit and welcome his conversation and comments. He is cautious beneath the affable front but kind, genuinely interested. He opens up bit by bit, around a calor gas brew. I feel he's been through some rough patches. This is recovery time, refuge.

Must remember to pick up some supplies today during the showers. He's eating me out of buns and biscuits. Sweet tooth – maybe there's a real old gossip in there somewhere too. But not the intruding type. He's relaxing.

Look at the sunlight slanting over that hill. A million wavelets come dancing into life. A shoal of fish cresting the sea. Not words but signals on the eye.

Infinite impossible eye.

I have been changing my walk in the morning to go down to the bay and along past Ms Lucy's cave. After the boats are landed and the catches tallied, I can still be in time to see her begin her day's work sketching and painting.

Catching the light when it is fresh as she will have it. She labours at her task without remission. For her it is more than work.

Next, I climb up on to the hill by Well Croft, where I look in on Mr David. He is mainly quiet these days and working on his reports, but he is courteous making cups of coffee on a little machine, so we are sitting for a while at the hearth and talking over former times.

He has seen more parts of the world than I had supposed. In that at least we are not dissimilar. Is it to be wondered at that he should sometimes be troubled in his mind? He does not speak of any ill health. He takes his own walk on the shore each afternoon when the sun is lower in the sky. And consults with the artist of our place. They are friendly now, in one another's company.

I am coming down as usual to the sands when I see the tracks – freshly marked with prints and scent. My good friends the otters are back, and I believe that old warrior Bodach is yet at the head. Every so often the greybeard leads his little tribe on migration from the inner loch to this, and then when he is minded back once more to quieter waters.

No doubt the visitors with their little boats have stirred him seawards again. For in his heart the old king loves solitude. To fish and then sport himself on shore and shallows with his harem and their young. He has seen a few seasons that greybeard king, yet here he comes again opening up his run.

Brigid will be pleased to know he is back, if I can be finding a way to tell her.

I must watch to see if he goes to the holts on Eilean na Cleirich. He avoids the seals, those voracious hunters, but the calving cows are swimming off now from the point, and the island appears deserted. Vacant territory awaits the next incursion.

We are very fortunate with this clear, moist weather. There is no drouth, yet visibility is good throughout each day. Coming back along the hill I see the clouds gather offshore and release their shower.

In the evening I shall sit at the gable end until the red orb sinks in his dying glory. At the rising of the sun and the going down of the same, the Lord's name be praised.

Could time myself by those clouds. Mid-afternoon they meet at sea, then roll in to freshen us. Something about routine.

You can't plan or dictate it, but once it's there you can drop into place. Feel the difference. Quite helpful, anyroads.

Even on the Darfur watch, amidst bloody chaos, there had to be a drill. Up soon after sunrise, then out with the chopper before the heat had time to simmer. Ground below parched but with glints in the early light – the wells, scattered trees. Eyes sharp, scanning for tell-tale smoke trails. Touching down now and then to check on surviving settlements, or on burnt out enclosures dotted with relief tents.

I'm going out each morning now. Sleeping better and fewer pills. Less dreams, or ones I remember. Head past the wood as far as the church, walk round it, not in, no sir. Then back along the ridge catching the morning views.

Then I come into the causie and go to the well. Lean down and connect my mind with its cool, deep shaft. Touch the rough stone cover with my forehead three times. Like a Muslim at prayer. It feels weird but peaceful.

Next, I make the coffee and set to work. After a while Donald MacLean comes in on his rounds, so I make more coffee and tell him what I'm trying to write about that day. And he always has a question or a point that sets me thinking. Helps me get perspective. He's seen a bit of life that greybeard. Once settled in he likes to talk man to man. It feels like Donald's gig, and he speaks as if I've been a soldier like him. I keep saying it's worse being an observer, passive, impotent.

Now, it's all building to the highlight. My afternoon walk and tea with Lucy. By the time I get there, Ulster tea is stewing on the gas ring.

Beneath showery cloud, reflected on the surface above, he swims towards the bay with silent underwater power. Putting his head above the surface in the north channel, he sniffs inquisitively, whiskers quivering towards the point. Then ignoring the remnants of the nursery, he turns without hesitation to the island.

Grounding, he works his bulk awkwardly ashore, seal out of water, and wiggles, drags himself ungainly up onto the rocks. Nose pointed up to the tumbledown enclosure and beehive cell, the eyes seem transfixed, shining in the wet. Muscles rippling up the throat and head, then back, his contorted bark or cry is recognition and remonstrance.

Irritated, the old dog otter slips off the rocks into the south channel. What unseasonable wind or tide throws up a bull seal here, when all the cows are calved and swimming westward?

'Aye, they're starting to slip away now. It's hard seeing them go, but something gets into them. When their mother sees the wee ones swimming, she just takes off.

'Are you upset by that, Bridie? You know the way of it. And your own gone long since. And mine.

'Aye, far travelled like the seals. You don't want to hear that.'

Tugging at my sleeve, she tries to form a word, nodding, with those strange seal-like whimpers.

'Listen, sister, share my loss and pain.'

She understands, calming herself to listen. Who knows what the spirits hold and hear, even when the mind has wandered. She has heard this story before, long since. But she wants to hear me tell it again.

'I saw my Abba grow up in the community of Fathers, like someone on the other side of a wall. When barely eight he left the women's enclosure for good.'

A sigh of satisfaction. We both want to keep what has happened near, in the present.

'I stayed on, a valued servant, always fetching and cooking and cleaning, on the edge of their devotional round. But he was my child, growing up in the care of those desert monks. He learned to read and write and fast and pray.

'Never amongst the women. We were the invisible ones, Bridie, handmaidens, yet I nursed hidden knowledge in my heart. Blessed be the fruit. Yes, we know that sign.

'But then the journey began, without reason it seemed or destination. I was terrified in those little boats, lost between huge skies and unending waves. But they ploughed through the water by oar or sail, always two boats, the band of brothers in one, and the followers huddled in the other, men and women.

'Eventually our boats nosed into a bay, through rocky islands to a green shore. And we arrived where we had left. Not the country I mean, but the circular walls and cells were just as we had left them in the desert. And the water in Ireland, Bridie, sweet and soft, clear and cool.

'I thought that we had reached Eden at the furthest ends of the earth, yet it was only a stopping place. Rest for a while, prayer and welcome, but then our journey had further to go. More stormy seas. Another bay, more islands and a deep pure well.'

Is that what allows me back? The uncovering of a well shaft. Bridie's silence.

'Have we been here before, sister? Dear one, I felt I should find you here, and that you would let me back in. That is what my heart has most desired. You know my sorrow as your own.'

Yes, the kiss of peace, placed on my brow. Re-united in the worn flesh.

Something shifted today; new phase begun. I think the trigger was seeing how the intertidal zone has migrated lower. Something about 'neap tides' at this time of the year making lower seas, MacLean told me. But that tiny adjustment on the big scale brings a wave of life change – multiple organisms burst out with fecund energy in the new space.

I want to record, capture that in some way, so I abandoned the drawings and built a rectangular wooden frame between the tides. From salvaged boxes, anchoring the sides in sand and observing everything in the exposed section: fragments of kelp and dulse, channelled wrack, a drift of sea sorrel, cockles and mussels, a scallop with limpets attached, two razor shells, whelks – different varieties – and a beautiful cowrie.

But if you wait and watch long enough, then you see flat-fish camouflaged against the sand, tiny crustaceans being left high and dry, burrowing anemones, sea cucumbers...Imagine it on the microscopic scale, teeming in miniature.

What could imitate that? A slow-motion film perhaps? I was transfixed, frozen, when I remembered the last little sketchbook Ian bought me. I ran for it, and quickly sketched some detail in crayon on each thick textured page. Then moistening it with sea water, I pressed something from the zone between the sketch and the newly turned page.

Later, Dave turned the pages cautiously showing a kind of impress on each reverse side – a seaprint. The results are mixed of course, but more importantly it opens up a new stream, a different kind of image combining organic matter with the medium – saltwater staining as well as freshwater colours......
Also I can repeat the framing, maybe with two or three simultaneous boxes so that I can catch different dynamics at different levels of the beach, in sequential stages.

Emerging, fermenting, decaying, being reabsorbed.

Dave began to look a bit phased himself, just listening to me spout on. Good humoured as ever though. Is there something else in his life apart from work that he would like to talk about? I should speak less and listen more.

Another exquisite evening. Eyes half-closed; sunset fluid on the retina. And then the stars begin to show.

Unlikely to sleep early tonight.

The Bodach has a big flounder on the shore. After a good fishing, he's feasting like Fionn Mac Cùil back from the hunt. Gorging himself, the old fellow.

Now he loses interest and swims away towards the point. What's wrong with his island holt tonight? Perhaps one of his wives is close by. He's one to be gallivanting despite the hoary head that is on him.

As soon as he goes the gulls come at his fish squawking and pecking in their hurry. They would sooner be scavenging than fishing on their own account. Unlike the waders there, and the oyster catcher who goes on unperturbed. Gille Brigde who hid Christ beneath the seaweed still bears his cross.

There is a story the old people told that the king otter came ashore once to marry a mortal bride. For he felt he was as good a hunter as any on the land. Besides he bore himself proudly and made a handsome figure with his fine coat and shining eyes.

So, he had his pick of the maidens of the country. And he and his bride lived well for many seasons, never lacking for the best of harvests by land or sea. But after a time, he pined for diving and swimming deep below the surface, chasing the salmon as sunlight glittered far above his head. He took up his old spoor and made for the sea.

Now his young wife sensed an escape - that he was abandoning her, and she called up the whole castle in pursuit, guns, dogs and spears. But he was ahead of them and alert to danger. In the frenzy of the moment, she urged them to kill rather than let her mate win free.

Now he was running for his life, the great king otter, but the missiles went this way and that as he raced and dodged towards the waves. Only at the last when he raised his head above the water for a last look, she hurled the dirk that pierced his breast. Diving down deep he shook the blade clear of his flesh, and then swam to Eilean na Cleirich, where he lay low and healed.

It was a bitter woman that he left behind, since her love had turned to hatred without any satisfaction being given. And one by one her children left her to join their father's kingdom in the sea.

Yet that is why to this day the otter has a weak spot, a black mark on the breast of his pelt. A blow struck there is sure to kill. Old wounds remembered, always ready to hurt anew.

They say that part of the MacLean bloodline comes of the otter. My cousin, the Bodach.

Tonight, I will be taking a dram for you, old one. Happy hunting to yourself and all our kin.

New fighting. On the radio. Christ, I thought better. Clinging to the chair, through a charred village, broken pots, one stray blue plastic sandal. Not a soul to be seen. Scorched earth, air and everything bloody else. The stench, sweating. About to gag, but no, don't back into that; I won't.

Make the coffee as normal, and start.

Head clearing, steady state. Finding perspective, Argyll style.

There's more than one war in Sudan. And more than one resistance movement in Darfur. That was the news - rebels in the south have started to fight each other. Accusing each other now of war crimes. Never mind the two million displaced, the God knows how many thousands dead.

It goes back to famine in the eighties. Khartoum arms the Arabs in the north to push out the Africans, so they start up armed resistance. Split on ethnic lines, yet they're all Muslims. And what does that remind you of? Aye, home sweet bloody home. Peace? So now we've handed it all over to the African Union to sort out. One Nigerian general with seven thousand disparate troops. As he states himself, 'I don't have wings and you say I've failed to fly.' Proverbs don't translate well in reports, especially African ones.

Am shivery this morning, even though the sun is already high when I wake up. I have slept badly. Two or three times I was out during the night, watching the tide advance beneath a three-quarters moon. Translucent, cool, but for me restless.

Perhaps yesterday left me overdriven, over heated, so there was an incipient chill in my system. So today the reaction is a slight temperature; wobbly, and reluctant to get up and begin the day.

Lying back, I ease over the pages of yesterday's marine prints, some of them sticking together. Is it only a mess of organic matter? What have I added to the process? Faster decay.

My attention turns to the paintings and sketches that are stacked in the cave, wrapped with taped plastic bin liners. What if the end result is the same? I see myself opening one package after another with sinking confirmation of my worst fears.

I am making a fool of myself, wasting my time and making Ian miserable. Is it because I don't want to share his family? I don't want to be a mother to his daughter. Not yet anyway. He is such a kind, loyal man, making no demands. Treading, warily in case I take flight.

Like I have, on permitted leave.

This is what happens when I do not focus one hundred percent on my work. I know that without complete concentration I cannot achieve what I am after. One morning off balance and emotion undermines me, with an insidious ache in the gut. And I am not about to get my period.

Pull back the flap and let the light in. A warming breeze. Perhaps if I drift into sleep, I can draw a veil. Wake up and start again, a different me, resolved. Not ill, just a little under the weather.

So, what's wrong with the weather? It's some other living thing I need today, a real interruption.

'It is a terrible thing, a great pity.'

MacLean sits by my (or his) fireplace, and gazes into the empty hearth. He seems distracted, not wholly following me on Darfur's multiple ethnic conflicts.

'A completely ruthless way to make war,' I emphasise, 'women and children targeted to eliminate the next generation.'

'That is the purpose, certainly. A terrible thing.'

Silence falls through the cool stone flagged room.

'I will tell you now about the chapel.'

'What happened there when...'

'What else should I be telling? It happened many generations ago.'

'How long might that –'

He was set on his own course.

'Many generations ago when the MacArthurs dwelt here, they were a proud, independent people, often at odds with MacSween on the other side of the loch. Now it arose that the MacSween warriors were wanted by their kindred in Ireland as mercenaries – the Gallowglass as they were known. And many went never to return, for the rewards were great, and they became the McSweeneys of Donegal and Mayo.

'Whatever the cause, their time of lordship here was coming to its close, and the MacDonalds wished to take their place. For Clan Donald, through its Lordship of the Isles, was growing in power. But the MacArthurs were in their way, settled with a prior claim and with a lineage that went back to Artur Mac Aedan, King of Dalriada. Though MacDonald took tribute from the mainland to the south, this peninsula acknowledged no sway, and that rankled.

'So it was about pride, not just power and land.'

'There is always pride, David, and the claim to honour. You must have seen that in Africa. What we like to call unreason may be allegiance to the tribe and its code of honour.'

'Not just Africa. I was brought up with all that in Ulster as well. Those McSweeneys were the paramilitaries of their day.'

'That is true enough, but in this matter there was no honour, just base cunning and murder.'

'How was that?'

'The Chief of MacDonald offered all the land from the modern village as far as the point to another clan. It formed part of an alliance with marriages and the ending of other feuds.'

'MacLeans.'

'Of Mull. Yes, David, my people. So a party of MacLeans came into the loch as if they were travelling to meet their new MacDonald allies. But this was a raiding party. Instead of feasting at Castle MacSween, they came ashore at the main settlement. The people had no chance. Some were cut down. Others, amongst them the women, children and aged, took sanctuary in the Chapel of Saint Abba.'

'In that building?'

'No, it was a rough-hewn chapel on the same site. The roof was thatched and the floor strewn with rushes. Fevered by blood lust, the war band set the thatch ablaze. It had been a dry season. If anyone tried to burst out, they were cut down and hacked to pieces. It is said that more than ninety people perished in the chapel that day.'

'A homegrown massacre.'

'Indeed, the intention was to leave no MacArthur alive.'

'That's how your family came to be here.'

'And yours remembered because of wider traditions, and the few who still observe them.'

'The MacArthur memorials. Maybe my family escaped to Donegal?'

'These were bloody times. You have no knowledge of your people's tradition?'

'Why remember bloody massacres?'

'Forgetting kills the victims a second time. I am sorry.'

'I appreciate your feelings, Donald, but these events are long gone.'

'Yet murder came to meet you at the chapel.'

'You think that I experienced...'

'I felt I should tell you. We live once more in violent times. I shall be on my own way now, David.'

And he does his usual trick, rising, inclining courteously towards the hearth, and then letting himself out.

For once I have no rejoinder, no farewell aside. He's taken the wind out of my McArthur sails. Back to earth with a bump. Which is crazy. It's all ancient history. But it feels part of this place, part of me, even now.

Time to get out for some more air, regain perspective.

He wasn't making that up to rattle me? No – it took some kind of effort to tell the story. He was primed up for it. A kind of admission, acknowledgement at the least.

So much for getting away from it all. Out of the fire into another frying pan.

'It's fresh out, Bridie, really beautiful. You would enjoy being out. The sand is warm beneath your feet and the tides low. Only a few seals left now on the point, getting the wee ones ready for a long swim. They've been getting away safely.

'It's bringing back to mind that first season we were here, so long ago. Do you remember any of that? When, we arrived after a stormy crossing, edging up the coast, one wee boat after another. Then we saw this perfect bay for the first time. With the island at its mouth and the ridge above. There were only a few people living here but we were made welcome for they already knew of the White Christ and his wandering poor.

'All the same it was hard to begin with. We did not have much food or fuel, only what we could gather, and we had to build shelters – the huts over the ridge – and the church with its turf roof and the Women's House by the old well. Then there was ground to till, carrying seaweed up from the shore, load after load. But by the time autumn came around again, with weather like this, we were able to rest and play for the first time in our new green place. You know, Bridie, how it feels to be able to say the word home. The bare, harsh desert seemed a lifetime away.

'And Abba was the leader now, my little boy called Father, though I dared not speak his name. That was the secret in my heart, Bridie, for it had the power, if let out, to destroy my happiness. Inside it was safe and joyful. But that is another story, sorrows kept like sealed jars on a shelf, for a winter fireside.

'Then I thought our wanderings were over, in this lovely place, our place, *mo cridhe*.

'Mind you there is some trouble with the young woman on the shore. I felt it this morning when I came by her tent. Something has disturbed her lonely dream, something of heart and spirit for I am sure she is not ill in body. Nothing serious anyway. What can we do for her, Bridie? You're the one that knows the plants and cures, like no other.

'Sometimes I think you've lived here forever. I'm just the incomer, a passing stranger. But you've always made me welcome at your hearth.'

'Are you alright?'

'So, so, but nothing life threatening.'

'I couldn't see you on the beach.'

'I slept badly. Think I got a cold.'

'You feel cold inside.'

'A bit shaky.'

'Not doing anything then.'

'Not so far. I stayed put in here.'

'Well, we'll soon fix that. See what I found along the beach.'

'Where?'

'The southern end. By the look of them, they've been in the sea a while.'

'I've never gathered so much. Fantastic, worn and grooved like the waves. Thanks, Dave.'

'Must be change of tides; different currents bringing in different stuff, from somewhere with trees or lots of wooden boxes. What will we do with them?'

'Put them back there in my store, in the cave.'

'No, I mean what can we do with them now?'

'What do you mean?'

'We could plant them, like cuttings between the tides.'

'See what pattern emerges. Dave?'

'Come on, don't give me an Ulster look. I've had more than my fair share of those over the years.'

'We could space out the planting, according to shape and size.'

'Whatever you say, Ms Lucy. Time to be up and doing.'

'Alright, ready when you are, Dave. We need to spread out, work fast to use the space between water lines.'

Shapes like branches, fronds, fragmented trunks, or brittle fences. How did I get into this?

'Mind the gaps. It's like a sea garden.'

'I'm a sea gardener.'

'This is art, man, you're making art.'

'Right enough, sticks do seem to stay upright, unlike some of the artists.'

'Don't push your luck, boyo.'

'Never fear. This is like being in on the six days before God took his kip.'

'At least he had one.'

'In the end.'

'Maybe we're near a Sabbath too. I need something to eat.'

'About time, I would say, and a wee glass of vino would not go amiss.'

'Whatever you say, Dr McArthur, whatever you say.'

Darkness has begun to creep closer on us. Then night puts on the lights of moon and star. Queen of the night, the old people used to call her. The joyful lamp of the poor.

It is not a night to be indoors as the old dog otter knows. Bodach has his own nocturnal paths and meetings. He hunts and does not go hungry, but he never disturbs the fishing unlike those foul accursed seals.

Taking myself down to the beach with a small refreshment I come upon a strange sight under the moon. In the middle of the bay below Ms Lucy's tent, there is a forest of sticks and weathered planks. They are being toppled by the tide as their hold is undermined. It is some madness of art.

Yet it is affecting to see those worn fruits of earth and ocean, taken back into the elements. She stands watching them tumble. Mr David is there also, and waves for me to come along. He and Ms Lucy are drawn together by this strange harvest. As I come closer, I see their excitement though she looks pale and tired.

'Are you not recording their fall?'

She gestures helplessly towards the lack of light, the sullen suck of the sea beneath the surface. I agree it is impossible to draw or photograph. Everything is under the sway of the moon. Perhaps this is not art but something much older and –

'What do you think of it, Donald?'

'It is strange and can never be repeated in this way.'

'You're right. Weird.'

'Will you take a dram?'

'I'm not used to having whisky. Oh dear.'

'Your good health, Donald.'

'*Slàinte!*'

'I'm going to sleep tonight for sure. *Slàinte!*'

The sun creeps slowly over the ridge as I wake. It seems to be rising later, and morning feels cooler till the air warms outside and inside my tent.

I feel a bit shaky again as I crawl out, perhaps for different causes. Same effect though.

At the tent's mouth I find a bunch of freshly picked flowers, or herbs. They are not like anything I have found on the seashore. Neatly bound with rushes, a special delivery to my doorstep. Yellow flowers with all their stalks and leaves intact. Where have they come from?

I take them inside and lay them by my headrest. Then pull the sleeping bag back over my shivers. Slipping into a doze, the early sun becomes a golden balm around my refuge.

I must be going along the beach early today. Ms Lucy was behaving strangely last night, and though Mr David was entering into the game, as if to humour herself, he did not seem his usual self. She may be unwell, feverish even, and a dram would not be the right thing to be drinking. The shore is no place for a woman to be on her own with no family to look out for her.

This light is very clear as if the showers may come earlier. And there was a first chill on the air as the boats came in. A big flounder lies half-eaten here, so Bodach has been at the fishing also. His tribe are feeding well on the seaward side so maybe he will be with us for some time to come. Despite the stray bull seal that is hanging around on the island. That one must be injured not to be at his breeding grounds.

Low waters again today, as the neap tide approaches leaving the shore rich in a sea harvest. The women would be out at this time gathering razor shells, clams and eels, enough to feed a multitude. And Bridget bowed by the weight of an overflowing creel on her back. Some years the tide went back so far they could walk to Eilean na Cleirich, stooping to gather as they went, like a row of gleaners behind the reaper.

I should be going out there to put the old bull out of his misery. End his line and the depredations of his kind.

I come close to the tent, listening quietly for signs. Yes, her breath comes light and steady – she is only sleeping. I could ease the flap and look at her fair, high-cheeked face, hair tumbled on the pillow.

She should not be exposed to any stranger on the beach. A Glasgow keelie, some clarty tink on the wander. Or a chancy landfall from the sea.

'Oh, Mr MacLean. Sorry, I think I fell asleep again.'

'No, it's I that am disturbing you. I only wanted to make sure you are well today.'

'Much better, thank you. Look, someone left me these.'

'Columba's flower. St John's wort as the English has it. A herb for healing.'

'Healing what?'

'A fever perhaps, or depression.'

'Is that what you think I have?'

'Ms Lucy, I am not thinking any such thing. I did not leave the bundle.'

'Then who did?'

'I do not know. The old people swore by Colmcille's flowers.'

'How do you take it, as an infusion?'

'The best way is to put the bundle under your arm when you sleep.'

'My armpit?'

'That is right. Then the body warms and breathes in its goodness through the open pores of the skin.'

'Well, maybe I should try it, even if I am on the mend. I am going to make some tea – would you like a cup?'

'Thank you, no. I must get back to the croft now. I may see you later.'

'Fine, thanks for checking up on me though.'

The flap falls back gently, and I turn to walk back along the shore. Who has been gathering the herbs and laying them at Ms Lucy's door? Those with such skills and knowledge are long gone from these parts.

Memories lost in Bridget's empty mind.

Gather Columba's flower by the moon. Go carefully on the banks by knee and hand to catch the golden glint. Nighttime is best when all the juices are drawn back in, the virtue concentrate. Go secret and alone.

As the mind sleeps gather flower, root and stem in a linen bag. Dream carrier.

New man this morning, after pure unbroken sleep. Must have been all that running up and down the beach. Like a ten-year-old building a palisade with bits of driftwood.

Still, seemed to cheer her up a tad.

That whisky found the spot – right down to the base of the spine then rising to the scalp like mercury in a thermometer. That was no ordinary whisky – where does MacLean get the stuff?

First time in years right enough, drinking for pure pleasure, the shared moment. But no sting in the tail. Christ, it's a new day. You go halfway round the world trying to find that moment, and here it is thirty miles from home on a deserted beach. The sun, and water of life.

Another of those bright, clear mornings you know will turn to showers before the afternoon is out. Like wearing lenses freshly shampooed and rinsed. Should be able to get down to work today. Session in the morning, then back to it in the evening still relaxed.

Can be done if I put my mind to it.

There's time though to wander down to the beach first. The tide's been way out – low water's creeping closer to the island but washing back in now. Not sure why the tidal currents in this sheltered bay are so strong. Something to do with the straits between us and the big islands. Time of the year.

She's up and supping tea, blanket round the shoulders.

'So, is this late breakfast or a brunch break?'

'Don't be nosy. And help yourself to a cuppa. I suppose you've written five chapters before breakfast.'

'Not a word. You seem to have perked up though.'

'I think so. Look at these.'

'What is it?'

'St John's wort, known locally as Columba's flower. They're a sure remedy for fevers and depression.'

'Jesus, so now you're a herbal healer.'

'Someone left it at my tent door last night.'

'Must be Donald.'

'He says not.'

'Local witch then.'

'It's healing magic.'

'Don't think I should try it though.'

'How come?'

'Probably has the opposite effect on men.'

'Drink your tea and don't...'

'Blether.'

'Exactly.'

Gulls wheeling and crying. Peep-peep of the oyster catchers and somewhere a solitary lapwing. Long listening.

'So, why are you here, Dave?'

'Sickie from the work. Nervous breakdown on service. I've three months to piece myself together for another tour, or I'll be out on my neck.'

'Tour?'

'Tour of duty, that's what they call these missions. Like I told you, conflict zones, peacekeeping observers. Standing on the sidelines, watching the damage.'

'That's rough.'

'Seems to be. But I'm working my way through it, out here in rural Argyll. The old homeland it turns out.'

'Are you on your own? Family... partner?'

'Not me. Was engaged once but she thought better of it.'

'All by herself?'

'Alright, there were reasons. I wasn't ready to settle. Anyway, what's this with the personal interview? Why are you here, apart from the Leonardo syndrome?'

'I'm in the same state as you. Not ready to settle.'

'And the reasons?'

'Not the man. Ian supports everything I do for my work. He's a treasure.'

'Must be. And the reasons?'

'I don't know really. But my father died, almost eighteen months ago now.'

'Sorry to hear that. Mine are both away, some time since.'

'We were a close family, Mum, one sister, Dad and me. Or so we thought.'

'But?'

'There was another woman, with three children.'

'Bit of a shock to learn that.'

'Dear Daddy, always busy, always working, but sometimes there, eager to kiss his darling daughter, his precious little Lucy. In between all that shagging.'

'You felt let down.'

'I can still feel his touch on my skin. And then I want to throw up.'

'Maybe he had his reasons. Sometimes men do.'

'Come on, Dave, don't make it worse. Every look, every kiss was a lie. How do you think that makes darling Lucy feel now?'

'So, what's with the art thing? Does that make you feel better?'

'It helps me forget.'

'For a while.'

'What does that mean?'

'Well, you can't live like a hermit forever, can you?'

'Because of Ian?'

'Fair play to the man, I never mentioned Ian.'

'Look, I know I'm being unfair, but I need some time, alright.'

'Don't get me wrong. I'm here for the same reasons.'

'You've a lot more reason than me.'

'Different wars; same casualties.'

'Dave, know what, you're quite a good listener.'

'For a man.'

'Mere man. Mind you, I think I could get working again today. I'd like to paint all those tidal trees we made.'

'They're gone, Lucy, vamooshed.'

'It's all about memory, pictures on the mind.'

'That bit I understand.'

'Come back later. Maybe we could tempt Donald to a ceilidh?'

'Dancing with MacLean?'

'No, stupid, a real ceilidh - storytelling round a fire with songs and music.'

'A wee social swallie, Hieland style. Sounds good. Can I get you anything at the shops?'

'Fine thanks.'

'Ok, take care. Don't overdo the lonesome genius bit while I'm away.'

'Bugger off.'

I am late coming to the Well Croft today and there is no Mr David. He will be on the shore tending to Ms Lucy.

It is better though to be on the ridge since the clouds have come in earlier today. They are drawn by the cooling of the air, the lessening of the sun's heat. Barely you would notice, but the neap tide is coming, and the year is gathering to its turn.

What a moon we have bathed in these nights, but now the Queen must decline once more and take summer with her. The creatures sense this and make ready. The deer will soon be swimming across the loch to assemble for the rut on higher ground. The geese will be heard overhead, though for now eagles and hawks still course their ground and lift what prey they can before the hard days ahead.

All things wear out. Treading the measure of this ridge, hill pasture, long dykes, forest, and the burial ground. Their chapel is deserted now, bare stones forbye the sorrowful ghosts and Mr David's haunting. The monks were not the first or last to leave their presence in this place.

There is time today to go further on. I can see the nine maidens of the headland. They stand as if an accident, pillars wading into the sea beyond the chapel and its sanctuary garth.

Druids went to make their offering at the stones - a hare, a solan, or a hind. Always the blood sacrifice, a cost for every gain in life. Nothing given; nothing won. That was the law observed by ancient custom, and it stands unchanged, unbending as these rocks, though disregarded.

Everyone learns in the end the price of their own having. They would wade out into the ocean and give their offering direct to Manannan, god of a hungry sea. And from the sea came life.

Life for life, and honour in the giving. Those remembrances are worn away, but the stones keep their ancient path out to the fast-flowing Sound. I place my hand on the sentinel rock.

My days are numbered. I am nothing. But in this pattern I am strong, never ending, as long as I hold fast.

'You know, don't you, this is my worst time. Give me the hard frost of winter, or the first signs of spring, but this, neither *tane nor tother*, as the year slips away. I busy myself around the seals and try to forget his going away from me.

'All those years, Bridie, I watched and followed, but not then.

'It began when we were at Moville. You don't mind hearing me talk? It's a comfort when you look at me with those soft eyes and take my hand. You're a dear woman, but this must be told and told quickly.

'Aye, Mara was her name. A true beauty, yet silent and withdrawn. She was highborn and longed to follow the White Christ. But her father had ordered an alliance with some other king – kings were plentiful in Ireland – and to seal the treaty she would marry a warrior son.

'She shrank from the marriage and denied her father. So, the young man came to the rath and took her by force. He imprisoned her in an underground chamber and then he came and forced himself on her. Again and again, until the insult of her refusal would be ended, by slavery or death.

'One day, with a hunting knife left by a slave who took pity, she drove her denial deep into his heart. And then she fled for sanctuary to Finian's enclosure. God knows she deserved refuge, yet I wish we had never set eyes on her face. But at the time I was drawn to her mute suffering. I held her in my arms in the Women's House, as we can, and listened bit by bit to her harsh telling. I was as close to her as anyone could be through her numbness. She was frozen, Bridie, by fear and shock, as any one of us would be.

'Abba went to see her too. And it seemed natural that in time Mara would come with us, leaving the trauma behind her. There was a growing bond between those two but also a keeping of boundaries, as was the way of the community between men and women. But when we came here, we were fewer in number than at Moville.

'And that was the beginning of trouble.

'Sufficient to the day, Bridie. That's enough for me, and you, dear, listening so carefully. I can't go on for now; it's time to rest. Who knows what another night may bring.

'*Beannachd leat, Brìghde, beannachd leat.*'

The moon is past full but still bathes the shore. It's colder, waning light. Go along past old Donald by the north end watching his otters, a whole family of them splashing in the calm waves.

Barely a breath of wind. And everything's quiet at the tent, sealed in sleep. Colmcille's healing work.

Then a muffled bark across the water, half cry, half plea, from the point.

Pick my way over the rocks till water is slapping on both sides. All seems deserted when between two boulders I find a blubbing, hairy pup. He's wailing softly, stuck, until with a hopeless effort to heave free, that cry breaks out again.

Looking round I see no sign of mother. Just this leaving. Stepping down I ease his rubbery flesh away from the sharp rocks and out he plops. Quickly gather him into my arms and hold close. I feel the fear ebb away and in its place exhaustion washes through him with a shudder, struggle for survival past.

Wrapping my shawl around us, I step carefully back over the rocks. A little mouth nuzzles, teases against my breast. This one needs rest by Bridie's fire, warm milk, a wool lined basket.

The beach is oddly quiet this morning. No sound of seals. The gulls and waders are out as usual, and oystercatchers feeding where the tide recedes. But I hardly hear them any longer.

Feeling much better today, though I have a strange recollection of waking in the middle of the night. I opened the flap and saw a woman hurrying along the shore with a bundle in her arms. It was cloudy but the moon was out, so I saw her clearly – white hair, shawled, stooping. Was it a child she was carrying, or even a seal? I went back to sleep. A dream, but if so where from?

Another bright day but the light seems softer, coming later. Perhaps it means the showers will arrive early. Out in the bay the sea seems a bit restless, gurly, but that may just be the tide going back through the narrows.

I have tried so hard to convey that motion, always latent but breaking to the surface, massing and tugging below to keep the face of the waters ever changing. Maybe it's beyond my ability.

Time to build again, creatures of the shore and tide. My boundary markers lasted two, three days in parts, but the conflict between land and sea is continuous. Millennia in the making, here at least. Must the sea always win eventually? Yet in that gap life finds its forms. And so must art.

My idea is to build a series of intertidal cairns, like the ones along the ridge of the peninsula above, but with more variety of shape if I can manage it. There is an endless supply of stones on the south side, though it will take a lot of carrying. These are the materials nature has provided.

Some of the cairns will stand spaced out along the shore, but there should also be a traverse line coming from the cave down the beach, aligned to the island. I'll settle each separate position as I go, no ground plan.

I feel extraordinarily calm about this, resolute. As if it is what my whole time here has been working towards, finding purpose in one monumental piece.

I am losing breath. My heart is fast because of the anger in me. Who did this? Bringing that filthy creature to my own hearth. Letting herself loose on the shore, a danger to her life. Who would do such a thing?

I must be walking more slowly now on the ridge, keeping my pace.

If that new nurse is involved, I shall have her dismissed by the Council.

Yet this is her own will, coming yet between me and the killing of those vermin. How can that be? Many's the time I would be clubbing them, destroyers of our livelihood. Or swinging their young by the tail till their heads smashed against the rock and brains and blood ran free.

People of the sea, cast back to the sea.

Now again she has a pup by the fire, defying my right. I made to take the creature, but she rose to stop me, whimpering, squealing like some bitch at bay. What visitant possessed – ?

I raised my hand. God help me, I almost struck her.

God forgive me her helplessness. It was that foul scrap of life. Not her. I would be losing control. Whoever brought that thing into my house will pay.

That is a cooling air on my cheek. Cloud is coming in now. Be my witness, I did not strike her. I must go to the stones.

'Donald, Donald!'

The Well Croft. Keep moving.

'Good morning, Donald.'

'Good morning to you, David.'

'Have you heard the news?'

He walks towards me out of the yard, face eager and open.

'They're charging him with war crimes, Al-Bashir the Sudanese President. It could be a turning point in Darfur, Donald. And for Africa, the international order.'

'I see.'

'Come in and have coffee.'

'I thank you kindly but – '

'No, come in, I need to discuss this with you. It's a turnabout.'

He is taking me by the arm and steering me into his croft. A seat by the hearth must hold my anger.

'He would visit the Well House, and we were often at the monastery. We were fewer in number here, and yet all the work to be done, prayers to be said. Cooking, feeding, growing, mending.

'I saw but I did not see what was happening. They were often together and there was comfort for both in that companionship. No offence or fault, Bridie, not then. It was remarked yet accepted. Till that day.

'Abba had withdrawn to the island, in solitary prayer and retreat. It was this season when the tide was low, and Mara walked out to join him. I don't know what possessed her to go. Some lonely unrest in her soul. But a wall had been breached.

'Of course, he should have sent her back, as our Father. But Abba never could refuse her mute appeal. They came back together after the next tide.

'He knew the mood, the change, immediately. He feared she would be driven out. Instead, he decided to leave himself, taking only his coracle and the gospel he had scribed at Moville. He told us the time had come for him to seek his own place of resurrection. Journeying, Bridie, far beyond this shore, to the ends of the earth if need be.

'He did not come to the Women's House to say goodbye. There was no protest or grief shown or reproach. It could not be mended.

'Three days after Abba left the autumn gales began. Seven days after he was gone, Mara went down to the druid stones and walked into the sea.

'Even Mary was able to hold his precious body. I am still waiting without news.

'I must cling to this place. You let me hold on till time recognises me. Some wounds can never be bound up, but it's the uncertainty that kills. Will he come back? I still hope, even to mourn.

'You see more, Bridie, than you can say.'

Himself seems a bit put out, flustered, agitated even, now I see him in the house. I put him by the hearth and organise some coffee.

'Boats all in ok?'

'Indeed, yes, the fine weather is holding. Though not for much longer.'

'How's that?'

'With the neap tide and waning of the moon, there will be a change. Most likely storms.'

'Suppose after the last week we can't complain.'

Weather dried up.

'So, what do you think about this new war crimes tribunal? Actually applying international law.'

'I don't know about the Sudan.'

'But you were in Aden, and Malaysia?'

'As a soldier, David. Men do things in wars – are ordered sometimes to do things they would not entertain elsewhere. Driven to acts that...'

'And we should condone such acts of war?'

'No, I have seen the terrible effects of unbridled violence.'

'Yet?'

'You are holding me to account, David, like this tribunal.'

'Sorry, you're right. I'm a bit tense today with the news of it.'

'Of course. I was in Aden, as you said.'

'In a difficult situation?'

'Two reconnaissance parties were murdered in the Crater. That is the centre of Old Aden, between the hills. We did not realise that the native army had mutinied so two parties were sent in. They had no chance. They were gunned down and then their bodies mutilated, dragged through the streets.'

'Like Iraq.'

'They were Argylls, my comrades.'

'What did you do?'

'Colonel Mitchell. Mad Mitch, so they called him. Colonel Colin Mitchell commanded the relief force. We re-took the Crater, brought out the bodies, and imposed martial law.'

'I'm sorry. I had no idea you were in the front line.'

'It all happened very quickly.'

'Was that the end of it – the mutiny was put down?'

'There were difficulties in restoring order.'

'Had to be – we were losing.'

'Colonel Mitchell was not inclined to be admitting defeat. I think I must go now, David. Thank you for the coffee.'

'No problem. Sorry I waylaid you.'
'The fine weather may hold another day.'
And off he goes. That's my lot.

It is hard sometimes to be listening to Mr David. His nerves have not recovered from his experiences in Africa.

There is a first hint of autumn colours in the wood, even before the winds. Soon the deer will come back, swimming across the loch to find the milder air and shelter on this lower ground. I shall take two or three, before they thin and weaken with the leaner months. Lying low in the bracken cover, watching till the creature moves willingly into my sights, then gently squeeze the trigger. Death moves with such ease from my hand, such speed.

I shall go into the chapel today and sit for a time to gather my thoughts.

I am not often inside these walls. MacLeans were not buried here before but taken back to Mull. Shall I bring Bridget to this ground with the village people, or send her away?

To raise my hand after all those years.

God will judge me, as He has judged before.

It is very quiet within this place. Yet Mr David brought out some shade of murder, lingering in the shadows, awaiting its due time. The flash of sun on blade, blood slashing.

Was it myself that was the weak point? Did I let my guard down without realising?

Behind the pipers in full battle order, Mitchell at the head like some demented warrior of the fiery cross. We recaptured the Crater on that first day for the honour of Mitchell's British Empire, and the newspapers.

But the hard combat followed, unseen, unreported. Street by street, alley by alley, house by house. Into backyards and cellars, every torturous inch of ground. No quarter given. We lost twenty more men, but for every life yielded we took at least four. There were many wounded, rifle butts and bayonets against daggers and swords.

'Don't hold back, boys,' was his muttered incitement. 'Don't forget the Crater,' his whispered curse. Only Arab blood would wipe away the Scottish blood they had smeared across the sand. 'Give them something back that will not be forgotten.' Night after night, under cloak of darkness we did his bidding, while by day he strutted for the press and ignored all orders from above. He was like a dog who would not release the rat until its every bone had been crushed between his teeth.

We were all the young warriors, drunk on killings and beatings. Crazed while believing our actions were driven by a righteous anger. But not the women, only men. I enforced discipline, respect from every rank. What does Mr David know of real war – kill or be killed? Darkness, blinded by sweat, starting at every shadow. It was not permitted under my command.

Nor is it now. They cannot come at me again. I am not on trial and stand on my own ground. I have refuge here. For every year since, I have been given sanctuary.

Alright, rash move to switch on the radio again. Lulled into false security. Then, wham, war crimes tribunal special. Still, sounds suspiciously like some kind of progress.

Couldn't settle back to work, though truth be told that report is getting itself written. Then along comes Donald MacLean, out of synch, flustered. Something's up. Then he gives me all that Aden stuff. Maybe the news brought back memories for him as well?

Had a bite to eat - the Dave McArthur early lunchtime sandwich special. Cold sliced sausage, bacon, sauce topped with a wee sprig of lettuce. Then dawdled down to the beach.

Low clouds rolling in a bit early today, more moist than wet.

Which is more than can be said for Lucy. She's up to the knees in a turning tide, tower building. Tower or maybe a lighthouse, broad base sloping to the top. And all stone. How the hell did she get those rocks down to the waterline? It's nearly as tall as her.

Wish I hadn't asked. In no time we were on the next project. An old-fashioned cairn on the upper beach. Rounder and broader at the base than the lighthouse but needing even more stones. When it comes to fetch-and-carry, I'm your man. It's my peasant roots.

Mind you this is Lucy at the top of her act. Woman recharged, full of go, and keen to fire up the minions for greater effort. Minion at least, though wouldn't put it past her to recruit some passing strangers, if any passed.

Surprising though how you get into the swing. Prise, lift, carry, stack, then back for another layer. Round ones, oval, oblong, grey and quartz, schist and dark. They all nest singly in the hands. Makes your arms longer too. And wetter as those clouds thicken into rain.

The sea is up and lapping round the lower tower, sucking, undermining the sand, but it is standing firm. The wee cairn's still well out of danger but I need to get it up a bit taller before the gaffer blows a whistle. No time for stopping when you're properly started. Lucy's hopping round in delight with the lighthouse, then sobers up to give a helping hand on the cairn. The hair's plastered to her face, which is streaming wet.

Eventually teatime is called. I stagger up to the tent and collapse, totally shattered.

'I'd better offer you something to eat, Dave.'

'Don't go to any trouble, please, on my account. What have you got?'

'Baked beans and tinned sausages.'

'God help us, bring it on.'

Then we're hunkered round the wee primus, brewing tea and simmering the nosh. What an afternoon. If I don't drag myself back up to the cottage and collect some booze, we'll be washed out to sea or suspended for all time in this hanging mass of wet. Whoever said art was the easy option, the cultural skive? Marx, who never carried a rock down the beach in his mortal.

I strip off my soaking, gritty clothes. God, but it is wet. Relieved to pull on some warm clothes and a dry jacket, when Donald appears at the flap.

'Good day to you, it's very wet.'

'Sure is, all of a sudden.'

'Are you alright in the tent?'

'Fine thanks, I've been building stone towers all day.'

'I see, it is a tower. Very good.'

'I was wondering, Donald.'

'Yes.'

'Remember you said that when the autumn tides are low you can walk out to the island.'

'That is true, Ms Lucy.'

'Well, are they low enough now?'

'Yes, the neap tides will be with us by the end of the week.'

'So could I walk safely to the island?'

'Of course, with a little guidance to be avoiding any treacherous sands.'

'Would you take me there tomorrow, or the next day, if the weather is clearer? Perhaps in the afternoon?'

'Indeed, but it had better be in the morning when the tide is at its lowest.'

'Of course, that's stupid of me. I would like to go to the island. I've been thinking about it off and on all day for some reason.'

'Very good, there is no difficulty. But if it is to rain all night, perhaps you should come to the house to keep dry.'

'Could I not move to the cave?'

'Indeed, the cave is dry even in the wettest weather.'

'That's what I'll do then. I don't want to leave the shore when my work is going so well.'

'That is fine, Ms Lucy. I shall say good evening and be on my way.'

'Thank you very much for your help, Donald.'

'Take care, the rain may go off, or be very heavy.'

Nothing to beat it, very best. A hard day's labour, then eating round a campfire – wee naked flame anyway – with the red biddie flowing. This cave mouth is a cosy bield, looking out on the clouds clearing overhead. Just a weak moon hanging in there, but a clutch of stars winks at us through the veils. Tinned sausages and baked beans, the feast of kings.

We've had all the relaxed chat, telling me about her family, and Ian, and how the big bad wolf story walked out of the closet. Then what she wants to know about is the women in my life. So, no lengthy revelations there.

I try to explain that in my line of work it's a few months here, then a few months there. Brief encounters are the order of the day. There's usually relief on both sides when time comes to move on again. Let's you focus on your own baggage, never mind the other casualties. Admittedly there are a few exceptions, but they tend to be the dropouts. Peacekeepers don't seem to be the marrying type.

She's not satisfied with that line though. Wants to know about the broken engagement. What more is there to say? Once broken, less said, and so on.

You see, Lucy, I had a close friend, Martin who was killed by an IRA bomb. After that, I couldn't settle. Alison was the kindest of women, but she belonged in Northern Ireland, and

I couldn't bide a place that let its brightest and best be wiped off the slate. And for what? Standing up to their principles against tribal taboos. It gets me going even now. So, I'm not going there, spoiling the peace.

Take what the moment offers and keep on moving. That's my motto. Don't dwell on what's lost, or can't be borne anyway.

Time to empty the bottle and add a wee nightcap. No Donald to share a dram, and the woman's tired herself out with all those questions. He's out there somewhere though in the restless dark. He's another of my kind, that has to keep moving even when he appears rooted to the spot. *Slàinte*, Donald. *Slàinte*, Lucy, and *Slàinte* to the whole McArthur kin wherever you are. Eventually the prodigals come home.

Aye, right enough. Wee peck for Lucy and off. Up those perfectly formed steps, onto the path, pinpoints of light domed above me.

Stand a moment in the dark. Waves fall one after another, telling me I also breathe on this rocky earth. Arms stretched out, facing the sea. I hear myself shouting to the night, till tears course down like rain. I am on the ocean, tiding out and away.

We are keeping our own company tonight, Bodach and myself, whatever else happens on the shore.

Darkness comes in many kinds. Big sea clouds are clearing from the north showing the mass of Jura black against the sky. Wind freshens, sea stirs, yet the night is calm. Soon there will be storms and tides to shake the earth.

She is quieter now too in the house, content with the little seal in its basket by her side. I could take the creature under one arm and cast it back into the sea with no harm on its head. But when I hear her whimpering softly in sleep I cannot. I closed the door on their peace to take my own way out.

There is a kind of peace here also. I listen for the waves rising, smack against rock, then fall back against each other time and time again. Or is that the splash of Bodach? Flipping to impress his ladies, and to coach their cubs. Life in the old dog yet.

Tomorrow I shall take Ms Lucy to Eilean na Cleirich. Her heart is set on that small crossing. The weather should clear one more day for her. And tomorrow night we can be gathering to share a dram and a story, as neighbours should. Not driven out alone by things we would not wish to tell one to another.

THREE

CHANGE IS IN the air this morning. Fresh, clear skies; the bay ruffled but unthreatening. And so many birds wheeling and crying as the tide recedes. The rhythm of this last week has broken. And I feel that in myself – the excitement of going to the island, like an outing. Days of work suddenly paused to let something else happen, something new. Where might that take me?

I spare little time for breakfast – tea and a stodgy roll. What will I need? Extra jumper, sketch pad, bottle of water and the camera. Still zipping up my backpack when Donald MacLean appears along the beach with that striding walk. He is carrying a big pair of waders.

'Good morning, Donald.'

'It is just the right day for the island. Please put these on.'

Obediently I pull on the waders.

'We must follow a straight path from the Cave of the Cross –'

'Is that what this cave is called?'

'Indeed, the Gaelic is *Uamh na Crainn*.'

'I had no idea.'

'A straight line from the cave through the centre of the bay to Eilean na Cleirich. There is a landing rock there for small boats.'

'Is that how St Abba went across?'

'He would go there often to pray alone. We shall find his cell on the island.'

'What about the women?'

As we waited for the furthest ebb, he seemed inclined to talk, like a guide preparing his group for the tour.

'No, Ms Lucy, not the women. Though the Well House looks out on Eilean na Cleirich, your cave was their solitary refuge. Yet I suppose they held before their eyes that place of prayer, a defence against unexpected evil, averting the power of the Devil.'

'It is hard to believe they never went there. Have you not heard of curious women?'

'Well, there is a story that one time a woman went out at low tide to join Abba in retreat. But that led to bitter disputes and his departure from this community.'

'Where did he go?'

'Further west most likely, but where is unknown to this day. Away from such quarrels and bad speaking. There is still a proverb which would be in the English "one woman to the island is like a stone dropped in the well".'

'That doesn't sound very encouraging. Are you saying I shouldn't go?'

'Not at all. I was only answering the questions you were asking. That is just the old way of speaking. Now we must set out if we are to catch the low tide. Keep behind me please. Everything will be easy till we reach the tidal channel and then you must follow my footsteps. I will guide you through.'

Down the beach we go past the half-finished cairn and my tower, neither of which attracts the guide's attention or comment. The sand feels firm beneath my waders as I follow down the slope. Then we move into shallow pools washing gently round and back. The water deepens gradually till it feels as if we are surrounded by open sea.

I stop for a moment just to look at the shore and ridge behind me. The points seem far away on each side. Suddenly out here it is all much bigger, and I so much smaller, like a tiny figure seen from a flight path high overhead.

'We are coming near the channel.' He seems to have sensed my halt without looking back. 'It will get deeper as we go in and there will be rocks underfoot. Just tread carefully and the water will not be above knee level.'

'What causes a channel here?'

'It is the way the currents come in round Eilean na Cleirich from the Sound. They are stronger even than the tide, for they take the tide's power and then drive into the narrows. That is why there is such great difference between high and low waters on the island at certain seasons of the year. It is the force of the currents.'

'They sound dangerous.'

'They are to those who cannot read their movements. We are quite safe at this time. But the island has always been known as a place of power. Are you ready?'

'Right behind you.'

I can feel cold rising on my legs as I edge gingerly down the shelf. The bed is a mass of rounded rocks. After no more than twenty, maybe thirty yards, we are coming up again. Close up the island is surprisingly high and steep, but Donald goes surely to a layered series of rock that provides rough steps, a kind of landing place. Soon we are climbing steadily towards the summit.

We have just left the bay, but quickly our senses are overwhelmed by the rush of a running sea, wind and wave. Though the island is not in reality high, it does provide shelter in its lee. Up here I feel like crying out with the energy of the elements, suddenly face to face with the towering bulk of Jura's primal, sacred rock.

'It's a completely different place.'

'The visibility is with us today - there is Islay stretching to the horizon.'

'And these are the currents.'

'Quieter for now. When the tide runs they surge northwards to Scarba. There beyond Jura. You can see with the binoculars. That is the edge of Corryvreckan.'

I peer through the glasses and can pick out the different cliffs.'

'Is it the sailors' nightmare?'

'The tidal surge meets the open sea there. When we were young and foolish we used to dare the edge, running up the Sound and tacking to try and catch the curve before the whirlpool broke.'

'For fun.'

'For the thrill of it, bored with the fishing. But we knew these waters from childhood. Truly Corryvreckan is fatal to the unwary, or if badly judged. When she turns in on herself there is no escaping. Many a sailor has disappeared, and their vessels were never seen again.'

'The anger of the sea.'

'Some say that the whirlpool destroys yet also gives birth. Abba's cell is below here on the north side.'

'Looking towards Corryvreckan.'

'It is more sheltered there. He had a small enclosure for growing herbs and kail.'

'Would he stay that long?'

'Long enough to need fed. Or he came back and forth. The wall shows skill in the building and much of it still stands.'

We turn off the low summit and clamber over rock and scrubby grass to Abba's hermitage. The circle of the beehive hut is there, though the roof has long fallen in. Donald is right about the wall which is jointed in at each end to the natural rock looping out thick and strong between. A thing of beauty. Only at the narrow gateway have stones tumbled. Inside there are nettles and turf.

Donald is bent down at the hut rooting amongst the stones and turf. He pulls out a handful or two of moss.

'Here is the spring.'

Pure, soft water begins to bubble up. I bend and scoop up a handful. It tastes mossy but fresh.

'It's good. I brought a water bottle.'

Abba's Spring they used to call it. People came across by boat to fetch the water for cures. That was before there were so many seals fouling the shores.'

'Do the seals come here?'

'Some each season. They have gone now to the breeding grounds on Rona and Sula Sgeir. But there is one rogue bull still hanging around. Watch out for him.'

'Is he aggressive?'

'You have to be careful of the bulls at this time of year.'

'How long do we have before the tide turns?'

'One hour and a half, though an hour would be safer.'

'I would like to stay on my own for a while and sketch. Will that be alright?'

'You know the way back yourself now. If I do not see you crossing in an hour, then I shall return to collect you.'

'Thanks. It's so restful here, a special place.'

'I'll leave you to your painting.'

'Will you come later to the beach? Dave is planning some food and a drink.'

'That is very kind. I will come along the shore, and we will hope the weather holds a short while longer.'

'Are there storms ahead?'

'It is usual at this time of year.'

He was off up the slope with a zig zag movement, then over and out of sight.

I take another mouthful of fresh water and settle beside the tumbledown cell. The big difference here is the smells. Back on shore I have my spring, my cave refuge, my rocks, but the sea tang is much stronger here, the air salty on my tongue. How did he see, touch, taste, think? This is his island with me as trespasser.

Looking round me, I start to sketch the grasses, the enclosure wall, shelving rocks. Just a way of thinking with the hand. Then you see little sedges and rockworts between the boulders – tiny hints of textured colour amidst greys or black. Sun and breeze lull the thoughts while hand follows eye. Did Abba drift and doze here... was he tuned into some other stream of thought... a kind of waking.

Stone is firm and cool against my brow. Very peaceful curled round the well rim, listening to deep echo of the sea, far away. I realise I can be empty, hollow like a shell. Curving to the sound of everything that stirs and moves beyond me, and nests inside me.

Three figures come into the Well House yard. White linen robes with heads thrown back. And on their shoulders, one on her head, they carry baskets to be filled.

One woman is tall – yellow-golden hair tied back, brown skin and vivid blue eyes. She is beautiful. The second woman is young also, but slighter, dark, long raven hair bound loosely in a leather thong beneath her neck. She has gleaming milky skin, eyes suddenly black above white bone. Is she the princess?

Behind her the third woman appears short and strong, broad in figure. Thick greying hair is swept back into a decorative coil. She is poised, light on her feet, while full formed. Her face is rounded but clearly modelled, brown eyes beneath arched brows. She might be a smiling mother.

They do not look towards me, acknowledging each other, adjusting baskets, shawls and sandals without fuss or chatter. Then in familiar habit they form one behind another and move off, tall fair then strong short and lastly dark princess. And I am going with them, to the shore to collect firewood, shellfish for the pot, and seaweed for their raised beds.

I know these tasks. Covering the path in easy rhythm, down the steps we go, and disperse out along the beach. I share the bending, gathering harvest, leaning into the load, adjusting to each jar on body, tug on strap.

Then screams begin. Baskets thrown aside, tipped, loads scattered. A boat, hidden behind the island, is cutting towards shore. Oars flashing, gulls screeching. Run, run to gain the Well House. Panic blind and naked, shouts, a warning bell, and sheen of weapons. They are on the shore. Strain every lung to win the gate, bar, close... late runner.

Too late, too long, stretched on the stones, hands tearing, clutching, scraping on the ground. Must push myself up against the grey force, brow stinging, eyes filling with pain... falling down the rock edge.

Top of the range this morning, and that's not just the better weather. Read through everything so far and realise I am nearly finished. Plenty of 'i's' and 't's' but the guts are there.

Conclusions? Nothing we don't already know, but puts everything back in perspective – the suffering, the causes and what can and should be done. Yet probably won't. 'Since the UN deployed alongside African Union troops, one quarter of a million more people have been displaced.'

Beginning to sound like a man who's not giving up. But not today, no sir. Today's for cairn building on the shore.

Serious manual labour. Fine, fresh, breezy morning as you look out, though those wee clouds on the tops are starting some dodgy business. You don't scare me, boys, we're going to raise stones whatever.

No sign of Lucy down there as I get moving. Strange to think of the footfall on this route, out of the yard, down the old steps, and onto the beach. They're all aligned with the cave, then the island. Our cairn and tower are just markers on the beaten path. Centuries of to-ing and fro-ing.

She must be on her trip to the island today. It's the weather for it. She's had that in her sights for days, and old MacLean does not forget. He knows exactly when it can and should be done does Donald.

Cairn all present and upstanding, what's built so far at least. Lucy's lighthouse upright and complete too, which is encouraging, given the effort ahead. There must be a diameter of twelve feet here, and I'm ten layers up. So how many stones have to be shifted to get, say, twenty, or twenty-four up, allowing for it narrowing towards the top... Of course, these rocks aren't even, but they seem to average out if I keep picking within a certain range.

I carry first – stockpile the materials, and then select and place from my heap. That way the two jobs can get into swing one after the other. Need to get my skills into flow, especially if I'm on solitary today. Each stone into its best spot, like eggs in a nest, only a hundred times bloody heavier. Jesus, why did I get into this art caper at the brute strength end?

Well, enough of the chat, McArthur, your mouth's bigger than your muscles. These stones are meant for moving. So, focus, carry, then lay. No rest until this cairn's complete, or you drop. And I hope my labours are visible from out on the holiday isle.

I am not sure she is looking at me, yet her eyes turn in my direction as if seeing. There is something calming in them, deep, deep blue like water in a well, sunk in puckered brown skin. The way she moves her hands soothes, with a soft pat, or stroke on her tweed skirt down towards the basket at her feet.

Another seal. And I am still shaking from the fright of the beast. But this is a little fat fellow, mewling and squeaking with content, not that huge bruiser. The grey bull right beside me, staring with luminous eyes, breaking me out of that dream. And I ran, panicking down the rocks with scrapes and knocks. God knows how I might have ended up, if Donald had not come to fetch me back across the shallows.

Just a touch of 'I warned you about the seals', with me in no condition to mind or disagree. Realise I am still gripping the mug tight with whitened hands. The tea is warming. He has gone for the nurse, but I have created enough disturbance already, in this sanctum for invalids.

Bridget seems to smile gently. Or just wondering what madwoman has come running to her fireside, gabbling about seals and islands. Perhaps she knows everything already, eyes turned inward on decades of birth and death. Abba's Island.

It must have been her carrying the baby seal along the beach, but how could she do that?

An oily salt whiff comes off the little one. That's what I woke to, raiders without warning. A bull from the sea. And I bolted, leaving my bag and sketchbook behind.

And all that fuss, Bridget's eyes seem to say, about the people of the sea. They seem to have no fear left, as if she has lived through these things before. Which gives a calming presence.

'I must have nodded off. You know what it's like with the wind and sun, the sea air. It was so restful, as if St Abba were still there holding the universe in his stillness.'

'Is that what those guys did with their time then, meditated?'

'I don't know, but that's what it felt like. I started to draw but that just slipped away too and then I began to see those women... in my dream.'

'Leaving you asleep, with the tide due to come in. Maybe that big bruiser of a seal meant to wake you up.'

'Well, he certainly succeeded. He was barely two feet away looking straight into my eyes.'

'Can you describe him?'

'Big, huge. Skin densely wrinkled and folded. Muzzle and whiskers grey, grizzled. He just seemed to balance on the stones, rocking flipper to flipper, a mass of compressed energy. For a second, I just eyed him, and him me with those liquid pools. Then he shifted, and I screamed.'

'Was he going for you?'

'No, I am sure of it. But when he turned it was with such a release of power and muscle. The shock of it. I ran and stumbled but fortunately I remembered the rough steps, and I was careful letting myself down into the water.

'Donald saw you coming.'

'Yes, I was keeping a watch on the island and wondering when Lucy would be making a move,' confirmed MacLean.

'But the bull didn't come after me, not like the attackers in my dream.'

'Did you see the seal, Donald?'

'He has been there for a while. It is not normal for a bull to remain at this time of the year.'

'Could he be looking for the lost pup?'

'I have not heard of that before. Sometimes the cows have to defend their pups when bulls become jealous and attack them.'

'Their own pups?'

'They are impatient for the mating season to come again. These are brute beast, not pets.'

'Men, same the whole world over.'

'There was something I noticed about the bull as he turned away. There was a huge scar on his left shoulder. It ran from his neck all the way to his flank.'

'A scar?'

'Puckered and twisted. I am sure of it.'

'There is a story, a tradition of Abba and his time on Eilean na Cleirich.'

'And?'

'Well, it is just an old story from long ago.'

'Yes, Donald, we would like to hear it.'

'As you know, Abba went to the island for periods of solitude and contemplation. There he was sufficient to himself with fresh water, his vegetables, unleavened bread and sometimes a line-caught fish. During one retreat there was a season of storms and conditions were harsh, for big waves can break right over the island's crest. Abba was sheltering in his cell, struggling to survive the cold and wet. Then to his surprise a great bull seal came into his enclosure as if seeking refuge from the storm. He lay down by the cell moaning in distress. Abba came out in the wind to see what was wrong, for he had no fear of the people of the sea. There was a long hunting knife embedded in the creature's shoulder, and the force of the waves was dragging it down extending the wound.

'The bull had surely come ashore to die. So, Abba drew out the knife, and being skilled in healing, he cleaned and anointed the wound with herbs, stitching as he went with the cord he used for a fishing line. The great seal let Abba have his way, despite the pain he must have endured, and for two nights of storm he lay there and rested. And each day there was a new dressing, but on the third day the weather calmed and before Abba rose, the bull had returned to the sea.'

'Was he ever seen again?'

'That is not in the story. I suppose when the storm abated Abba would have come ashore to replace the supplies he had lost.'

'He was wounded like my seal.'

'There are wounded seals, then and now, though perhaps from different causes.'

'But he might have come to warn you.'

'I just hadn't thought of it that way.'

'They are clever and cunning.'

'It's been a strange kind of day. And that dream. They were all going with empty baskets to my beach.'

'Women went each day to harvest the tides – shellfish, timber for the fire, seaweed and wrack for the soil.'

'But something happened on the beach, an attack or invasion, and they ran for their lives.'

'What happened – were they caught?'

'I don't know because I was wakened. Could that dream have been based on something real?'

'There were often raids on this coast from Ireland, and later from the Norse. Even Moorish pirates came here. They took livestock, crops, goods, but their most valued prey was people, to be sold into slavery. When they were not strong enough to attack a settlement, they might snatch women foraging on the shore. They took children too.'

'Those were women from the Well House. I seem to have dreamed into an old fear.'

'Not so old. That's exactly what happens in Darfur. The women go out from the enclosures to fetch firewood. Then they become targets of rape and murder.'

'To destroy the tribe. Clan on clan.'

'MacLean on McArthur.'

'What do you mean?'

'Genocide. Yet the raiders were after something different, to trade flesh rather than destroy it. The women became their property to use, abuse.'

'That would be the way of it. These were dark times.'

'Aye, but we're still at, enslaving, murdering our own kind, and no-one's prepared to stop it.'

'You've done your bit, Dave.'

'I've finished my report, and I give the last word to an elder from the Hansa Hisa camp. He's a man like you, Donald, full of years, knowing all the stories and traditions of his people. But he's been broken by our failures to prevent their destruction.'

'What did he say?'

'Every day women are raped, men killed. The United Nations cannot reach Hansa Hisa to begin patrols, but they came to report. They put up a tent outside the camp and the Janjaweed took it down. We are on our own.'

'The night is cold. Shall we have another dram, or are you ready to turn in?'

'You saw the cruelty of war, Donald.'

'Indeed, I was in action with Argylls, in Palestine, Borneo, Malaysia, Aden. There was cruelty on all sides, but we did not target women.'

'I'll have another, Donald.'

'No Argyll killed a woman or a child.'

'But you put the fear of God into them, like Lucy's women running from the shore.'

'It was not right, what we did, what we had to do. It was not right, David. And that comes back to my dreams yet.'

'I'd better have that dram, if it's still in order, Donald.'

'Indeed. We do not stand on ceremony here. Not tonight.'

'*Slàinte.*'

Waking late from a sound sleep. Taste of whisky still dry in my mouth. Everything grey out to sea – down payment for early rain. Made a lazy breakfast with orange juice and then several cups of coffee.

Something stuck in my brain about MacLean's accounts of Aden. There was something missing. And he shut the subject down hard and fast last night. Too close for comfort you could say, and not just for him. Demonstrations, outbreak of savage violence, searches, women and children screaming.

You get that feeling sometimes with witness statements. An important part is held back, too far back or down to be brought out or shown to a stranger. Someone who had not been there, who could not understand what it had been like or why it happened.

Need to switch off. Maybe I'm imagining this – still report writing. But that bit is nearly done, and real work requires attention. Tip everything into the sink, pull on jacket, woolly hat, and head out.

The grey seems moist and warm again, but just as I come out of the causie some movement in cloud cover reveals the island, bathed in watery light. Like some ancient boat adrift in the mist. By the time I reach the steps it has gone out into the banks of ocean.

Whisky is definitely not my drink. Must have tossed and turned, leaving me tired and light-headed. Now everything seems to be resolving into one last big effort.

From the tent door, Dave's cairn is directly ahead, half-finished but upright. Next in line is, or was, the lighthouse undermined by the suck and tow of the tide. Half collapsed it looks more like a tumbled cairn, still pointing towards the island, muffled in grey mist.

The day's raining in that soft, wetting way it has when the wind is low. Everything is in transition between sea and air, sand and water, earth and stone. The missing element is fire.

What I need are three fire beacons on the tideline, built from stone but more squat and solid than the lighthouse. Like Dave's cairn but with a hollow basin at the top for wood. They can be lit as the tide comes in and then keep burning as the sea rises round and darkness falls, red breaking black from black.

The line of beacons runs from towards the arms of the bay, traversing the cave to cairns, and echoing the reach of Eilean na Cleirich across the bay. This encompasses all the work to date, in preparation. The beacons complete the series. I can photograph, sketch and video the beacons to provide a centrepiece for my exhibition.

I'll need Dave's help though, so I hope he's not hungover, or fed up with shifting stones. Perhaps Donald MacLean can be persuaded to organise fuel for the beacons.

One last big push. If it works then everything has been worthwhile.

'He'll be ready to go soon, the wee darling.'

With short high barks he waddles on the floor, stretches up his rubbery neck towards the woman inching behind him with stiff and painful steps. She moans and whimpers in unison with his cries.

'Yes, sure it is, he'll need to go. Come and take your tea before you fall your length.'

She settles back into her chair beside the hearth.

'It's a good cup, Bridie, the very best. And do you know they're ceilidhing down on the beach. They sit in that wee tent, while the sea grumbles outside. Now that brings life back to the place. After all those who are gone – songs, prayers and blessings gone with them. Yet the tent gives out a circle of light. Even himself is there, not knowing, though he thinks he does, all that went before or what might be to come.

'Don't worry so. It's a good cup, Bridie, the very best. The winds will be with us soon, so we'll need to get the wee fellow launched before it gets too rough. I know, Bridie, we both ken his time.

'You'll miss him, but it has to be. It's my bad time too, with his going at this season. What happened to my son, Bridie? Sometimes I think you know more than you let on. Did he go to the bottom of the sea? Is that why he never came back? It may all end in the cold, murderous ocean.'

Squeals and barks.

'Not for you though, my pet, not at all. The waves are your home. Can we ever be at peace? Mary Star of the Sea, bring us to safe haven. Bring the voyagers home.'

Three foundations laid, and you can see the pattern. It works, it does work.

Dave is like a man possessed. He seems to have developed a technique for choosing, carrying, stacking in one flowing movement. He doesn't look strong but he's wiry, tougher than he seems. And he's completely focussed, everything else forgotten. It's me who is half attending, half looking on.

We are getting progressively soaked but it's not cold rain and we don't seem to notice. Tea break, then I will have to let Dave finish his cairn. He wants to know if he'll be credited with copyright for that piece of the finished series. Men. Everything has to reflect back on them. But he is kidding, I think.

The sea is very calm. There is something still and waiting beneath the water. Even the stones are silent. We do not bring offerings here any longer, but today I will leave the bracelet.

Everything I told to Mr David was true. Closing in on the Crater after the ambush, picking off the resistance with snipers. Each counting in the tally against our dead. And then Colonel Mitchell's invasion force – pipes, photographers and armoured cars. We recaptured the public buildings and established our camp in the centre of the old town. Stirling Castle we called it, with the Union Jack and regimental colours raised above.

But then the real work began, out of sight, alley by alley, house by house. We lost eight more dead in there, including Billy Orr. We joined together, he and I, served together. Then he was gone. There was no official record of enemy casualties, but we knew how many we were taking for every one of ours. That was more than I could be telling.

It is a trinket, with many links such as all the Arab women wear. But in this bracelet the chain is broken. I do not know why I took it from the ground, as if it were a piece of evidence to be hidden. Just one more bit of debris in that room yet somehow part of herself, violated.

They said that she was willing. McLaughlin, Thomson, McAlister. But they were three together beside her wails and tears. It did not seem right. She was not a whore. I drove them out, but she was inconsolable. I had come too late, and I left her in that state. There was nothing more that I could do to help her.

I could have called an ambulance. There were only two operating in the Crater. Once a doctor had seen the woman's condition, it would have become an exploding grenade. Accusations, investigations, charges. The regiment shamed, perhaps withdrawn, when everything depended on us to regain lost ground. Even though an empire had been lost, blood for blood. I thought of telling him, but I knew Mitchell would look the other way, and blame me for not doing the same.

I kept the bracelet, a broken chain yet a pledge I had not forgotten. Two days later the nationalists shot her as a collaborator. They said she had shamed her religion and her people, and that all traitors would be dealt with in the same way. Then I knew we were losing, for all Mitchell's heroics. We had become an occupying power, the infidel oppressors.

I should have told Brigid. What it was like to shoot a man, to see a comrade blown to shreds, to see a woman abused and desolate. I built a stone wall between us. That was the beginning. I had fought so that our home might be preserved, so why besmirch its tidy warmth. The other had been foreign land.

I let the memory fester, and sometimes it erupted. There is always a price, but I should have been the one to pay. Brigid was cowed by terror of my rages, and I drove away our children. I see it all now, as she must have seen it, yet it took a stranger with his tales of Africa to bring truth home.

There should be sacrifice to restore the law of life. After so many lost years I lay this pledge on the stones. My promise to uphold the ancient ways of honour and of healing. I shall bring the broken to their mending.

Powerful. That's all you can say. The work we put in today. My cairn fully crowned and the bulk of three stone beacons built as strong as the Giant's Causeway. Yes sir, and despite the rain. No surrender. Powerful is the word.

Tonight nothing is left to chance. No baked beans and tinned sausages for us, not after the work rate we've clocked up. The village shop has surrendered its best meat and veg. This is the night for Irish stew according to my own special recipe, supremely flexible depending on available ingredients. There has to be some payback for the bachelor life.

Bittie of garlic, diced not crushed. Steak into the fry pan with a full-on sizzle. Then onions and peppers into the foot of the other pan, all elegantly sliced. Now, just when they're both nicely on the turn, tip steak into the veggies with one clean move. Let them sizzle again together. Quick swallow of plonk.

Next, two tins of tomatoes, one of pasta sauce (alright, that's cheating but who's to know and it saves on herbs) and as it comes to the boil half a bottle of red wine. Savour to taste. Cheap plonk of course but I can drink the rest and save the good bottle for dinner alfresco. There's no refusing a man who's done his duty, and much more.

More salt anyway. This meal would satisfy anyone from God to Donald MacLean and all the women in between. Don't suppose there's a bay tree round here. Mind you those Well House women would have had their herbs flavouring everything, with a bit of healing kick amongst all the shellfish – venison for feast days. Not a patch though on your Irish beef. Get a whiff of that. Torn now between sloshing in more biddy or drinking it. Time to lower the gas a tad.

Now I can lower my aching arse gently onto a seat. Breathe out. This art thing gets to your body not just the soul, or mind, or whatever. Anyway, here's to them all – best of plonk.

'Delicious. You're a man of hidden talents, Dave.'

'Modesty forbids. I only have one recipe – casserole. Chicken, fish, meat, whatever, I just add the same ingredients.'

'Well, it works. And the wine is lovely. I owe you.'

'Better than whisky? It all depends on the temperature. We're soaked through today but warmer. No sign of Donald though, dram or no dram.'

'Maybe he's brooding on all that old stuff about Aden. You could see him tensing up. No woman touched or offended.'

'Perhaps. He's been on the rough end for sure.'

'What about the women?'

'Bad news for people trying to keep normal life afloat, wherever you go. He may have spared us the worst details, old Donald.'

'How come?'

'Don't know. I just felt there might have been something more to tell. He was holding back.'

'Says the big confider. Sorry, Dave.'

'Relax. I know I'm buttoned up; it's just the style of clothes I like to wear.'

'Self-knowledge, they say, is the beginning of wisdom. Mind you there's been plenty to think about these last few days. What happened to Abba?'

'Where does he come into it?'

'The seal, stupid, the bull seal. I can't get him out of my mind. That scar.'

'Ah but the seal always comes back.'

'Sorry?'

'It's in all the stories, back home in Donegal. Man helps seal, so seal helps human – rescues him from drowning, shipwrecks, tide traps.'

'So maybe the seal helped Abba, on his dangerous voyage.'

'Could be, if help was needed. Maybe he came ashore on some remote northern isle, and a good woman took him to her bed. End of story.'

'If that's what he wanted. But there could have been another hermitage, much further out, besieged by wind and waves, with only seals for company.'

'Or he kept wandering – the stone that gathers no moss, seaweed anyroads.'

'I know it's crazy, but I feel that seal was still looking for him.'

'Back across time. I thought he was looking for the lost pup. We need Donald here to explain. He'll have a story on the matter. Where can he be tonight?'

'Home with his poor wife I hope.'

'I didn't meet her.'

'Bridget. She's confined to a back room, beside a quaint old hearth. She has dementia, poor soul.'

'It'll come to us all.'

'Perhaps. She's still herself though in some strange way, connected. I felt that.'

'Here, you finish this.'

'Share.'

Last of the bottle half fills both glasses; no longer expecting another guest. Evening slows to rest. Conversation pauses. Warmth gathers, even as the night beyond defines itself sharper and clearer than we have seen so far.

Sleep waits for the long time being.

'Do you want to hear what set me wandering?'

'I've been wondering for weeks now.'

'Aye well, I don't make a habit of it. But Donald got me thinking.'

'About Ireland?'

'Northern Ireland. I was brought up in Londonderry, Derry for short. We were Protestants but not the bigoted brigade. My dad was brought up like I told you in Donegal, over the toy border.'

'They weren't toy guns though.'

'Anyroads, I was still at school when the civil rights thing began. And I had a pal, Martin. He was well fired up with the whole thing, so I tagged along. Marches, banners, public meetings kind of stuff. It wasn't just Catholics, though they had most to protest about. We wanted a new society in Ireland, north and south. God, we were hopeful.

'We did everything together, Martin and me, except shit, my dad used to say. Martin was the best – stood out for looks and brains – and where he went, I followed. So, we both went to Queens, the university in Belfast. He was doing politics and I did English Literature – softer, less edge, but I still kept up with the protests.

'Things had boiled up by now, turned ugly, rancid. The police lost it, went on the rampage in Catholic areas. They had to send in the army – the Brits. At first people put out the flags to welcome them in, but that went sour as the squaddies went after the IRA. They were still on the edge then, but making their presence felt.

'It was heavy-handed. House searches street by street; guys dragged out at night; martial law. Began to look like the local militia all over again and worse. Then came Bloody Sunday in our own dear Derry. Thirteen demonstrators killed by the paras and not an IRA gun in sight. But that was the boost those boyos needed. They were the defenders now, heroes and martyrs. Recruits flooded in. Civil rights were Catholic rights now, Irish rights. We didn't see it then, but a war was starting up, a dirty war.

'I came back to Derry to do my teacher training. By now the place looked like a war zone – roadblocks, barbed wire, troops on the streets. Folk in both camps felt under siege though somehow life went on.

'Martin was still in Belfast. He had joined the civil service on some fast-track thing, highflier. But he kept in touch, coming over most weekends. Alison was on the scene by now, a steady date, while Martin was, well, best mate. All seemed quite snug at the time.

'This Saturday we were up town. Had a sandwich and beer or two at McGilligans. Then we split to meet up later. I was headed for a bookshop up near the church, he was going to the Guildhall to pick up a leaflet about something or another.

'I'd only reached the Diamond when there was a thump behind me. Not a bang – more extended, contained. People started to run. I froze. Realising it was downhill, I turned and walked back. I couldn't run.

'It was carnage. Screams, glass, stone, bits of buildings. The Guildhall was trashed, blown out – you could see it through the smoke and dust. That's where the bodies were, nearer the Hall... parts of bodies.

'Dave, you don't need to go there.'

'I'm alright, Lucy. He had a green anorak on, trust Martin. That's how I spotted him, lying like a rag doll, something thrown away in the street. He was chalk white, broken. I got down beside him and cradled the limp thing in my arms. When the ambulance guys arrived, they took us both. I couldn't let go. No breath, no pulse, no movement. Prised us apart in casualty and took him to the morgue.'

'I am so sorry.'

'It was like being in a film, feeling nothing, but going through with it. Family grievings, public outrage, funerals. As if the whole town was dead and silent except for the foot beats of the walkers. Standing at Martin's grave, still not realising that what we were lowering down was the last I'd ever see of him.

'There was no sense in it. I gave up the teacher training and volunteered for overseas work. Then I drifted into the peace-keeping stuff and somehow stayed with it. I knew it would take me out of Derry and it seemed to be something I could do. I became a wanderer, just going back occasionally to see family.'

'So, you broke up with Alison.'

'Had to let her off the hook. She was facing a life sentence.'

Head bent over the glow of the stove. It sputters on gently. Slight, flattish with the short fair hair cropped, greying from the edges. Can't see the downturned face but you feel the sadness.

'What comes next?'

'That's partly why I'm here, to see if I can still hack it. Then back again I go.'

'Darfur?'

'Darfur, Congo, South Sudan when it blows again. Somalia if we ever get back in.'

'Or try something different?'

Just the hint of a shrug, my hand could touch. Stroke the back of the head, neck, shoulders. Something seems to hover between us for a moment. As if another person was there, willing the nerves to move my arm.

'I should be on my way.'

'Well. Thank you.' The shadow rose behind him. 'And for all that incredible work. I couldn't have done any of it without you.'

'Don't speak too soon. We have to finish the job tomorrow.'

'I know, but we're nearly there. I'm sure of it.'

'You'll need to be the torchbearer – ceremonial firelighter.'

'Maybe, but I promise I'll also be chief cook.'

'Would that be the tinned sausages recipe?'

'You'll take what you get and be grateful.'

'Alright, see what the day brings. Sleep well.'

Touch on the cheek and he's in the dark, black shape receding up the steps. Gone into night.

Back in the light of the stove, I don't feel like being inside. Pull out my sleeping bag and curl up below the flap. A pillow, Columba's herbs. Underneath bright stars, safeguarded by the quiet wash of waves. A half-moon rises perfectly accompanied by its shaded hemisphere.

Watching. As eyelids droop. I remember to roll back and douse the flame.

The old one has flitted, moved on, leaving no fresh tracks, no scats, no half-eaten dinners. And on such a gentle day, with tonight's half-moon rising. He knows, the grey-muzzled rogue, what this stillness means. Beneath calm water he feels the far-off storm stirrings, so he migrates without a backward look, and the little tribe goes overland after him.

He cares not, wise Bodach, for this place or its people. All he wants is ease of life, fish aplenty, and sheltered space to play. One shore will do as well as the other. He has another generation in him that old dog, unlike me.

I could have gone along the shore tonight. When I heard their murmuring voices it was an invitation, but I would not have added to the company. I should have taken my place at Bridget's fire, and before winter closes in, I shall be present there again. But while that stinking little seal is beside her, I cannot abide the place. And she will not abide me.

Yet I owe her those lost years, even if she cannot understand my intention or her recompense. Those vacant eyes. Something moves behind, or she would not defend her cub so fiercely.

Perhaps tomorrow if sleep comes kindly, I can start again. For now the *uisge bheatha* fills my empty shell. This old fellow warms me, golden like the moon. It builds a path across the bay for me to walk. Stars overhead to guide. Following that bridge I could go over the edge of the world. Falling into the dark, as a soul is sucked into Corryvreckan never to return in this life.

FOUR

MY LAST BIG day, and everything is conspiring against me. Woken in the night by canvas going taut, then whipping back. Wind and rain worse than anything so far. Squirmed into more clothes, without leaving my sleeping bag. Couldn't get to sleep properly. Morning and it's still blowing a gale. The weather wants to drive me off the beach.

For the first time in weeks, I feel that knot of tension in my guts.

The day's tasks. Just the tops of the beacons to finish, as long as the wind hasn't disturbed the top layers. I can see the main structure standing firm. Cairn capped and complete before my eyes. It's the centre of the whole scheme, guardian amongst the elements with the beacons spaced out like shoreline sentinels.

We can't be stopped now, but I need Donald's help with the fires, especially if it's going to pour all day. I'll have to move everything into the cave first to keep dry. Surely it can't rain all day.

God, I promised to cook. Can't believe I heard myself saying that. I'll need to fry steak, sausages, bits of chicken, like a barbecue; get some salad stuff to balance it up. Plenty of tea and coffee left. Buy some chocolate and drink. Not much of a wine selection in the shop, and whisky for Donald. What kind will he drink? |Ask the shopkeeper. When will I have time to go to the village?

The video has to work, even in the rain. It's bound to let up by evening, clearing. More like squally showers passing over, a series of squally showers. Uninterrupted series. Listen to them. Five-thirty am.

Unzip a few inches for another recce. Banks of grey cloud like giant waves. Impressive in their own way. The bay is a cauldron of white crested snakes. Island almost submerged, and that first construction of mine, even the remnants, completely washed away.

Tug the zip back. Give it another hour, huddled into myself for warmth. I'm not ready to get up quite yet. Hard to believe that my time here is almost over.

Weather broke on us, but I missed the big event due to deep and dreamless sleep. Must have been the whisky. No half measures. Rain beating on the windows and wind scouring round house and yard like a demented besom.

Hope herself's tent hasn't blown away. Peer out to get the picture. Big clouds scudding over the islands. Big waves running up the Sound, even in the bay. Pull on some clothes – this is cold. Atlantic precipitation as my old geography teacher would say in full throttle.

This is serious if Lucy's sculptures are to get finished – it's her last weekend. On with the fire. Another jersey, two pairs of socks. No surrender, but a fry-up is definitely in order before facing the beach.

What a lovely woman she is – a looker but much more. Genuine warmth. So how come Ian's at arm's length from Argyll? Lucy's been cutting herself off – reasons of her own, for a time. It's that artist thing in her. Not sure I really understand the woman. But who am I to criticise, a fellow fugitive?

'Recent arrival? Mars?'

'Very funny – I might say the same about you. The plastic bag's very fetching.'

'Keeps the rain off though.'

'Thank God something does. I've had to move all my stuff into the cave. It's dry in there but musty.'

'How about the edibles?'

'We can worry about them later, after we've got some work done.'

'Fair enough. I might get anxious though as the hours tick by.'

'Point taken, Dave. I won't let you starve. I couldn't have managed this without you.'

'Ok, enough of the touchy-feely bit. Lead a man to his rocks.'

'Right, I've got a sketch here in the tent. This shows how the basins at the top should look.'

'I get the idea. Not a problem. I've got enough loose stone piled up at each beacon. Should finish the job without fetching and carrying.'

'We can't have long. God knows what effect this wind has on the tide levels.'

'I've got my wellies on. Seriously, if yesterday's work stood up to the pounding, then we're nearly home if not dry.'

'It's all there; you can see for yourself. Only my first construction's been washed away.'

'Built on sand, my dear, not far enough out.'

'So, you were taking notice.'

'That's why I pushed the middle one further out than the others. There's stone on both sides of the bay, but here you have to go deeper under the sand.'

'I didn't notice.'

'You're the one who walked out to the island, Lucy.'

'You're the one who's missed his vocation. Light-house builder.'

'Well, are we doing it or not?'

'Is there a choice?'

'We're too far in, no going back.'

'Are we taking one each, or working together?'

'Together I reckon, so you can pass, and I can build. Keep the master mason supplied.'

'I'm the designer remember, the artist.'

'Right enough, I'm the navvie, as long as the tea breaks are regular.'

Spun by the wind; shelter in the lee of the towers, and doggedly stone set, layer by layer. Water running over your face, down your neck, up your sleeves. Tides sucked beneath those big waves.

Hold your ground. The wise man built his house upon the rock.

The boats have come back early with light catches. They will not go out tonight, or for several nights. The wind must have woken Bridget, or that squirming creature. It will have to be going back to the sea now, and she knows. This is only the beginning of storms.

Our visitors are not realising. When I trained the glasses this morning on Lucy, she was crawling out of her tent to check on the structures. She and Mr David are preparing to complete them today. She thinks her time in the bay is coming to its close, but the weather may be against her.

As I come along the shore, he is playing the fool, hopping in the surf, flapping his sleeves like the wings of a bird, a shrike. But he sets a good stone, does Mr David. That will be the MacArthur in him, skilful and cunning, if sometimes deceiving. Nothing so old as the hills, the devil, or MacArthur.

'How are you, Donald? What a terrible day.'

'There is enough rain in it, certainly.'

'We're going to need your help with these beacons.'

'The beacons are to be lit today.'

'It's essential – they're the crown of everything I've done.'

'We'll be needing some peats soaked in paraffin. No kindling would survive such a downpour.'

'Surely it won't rain all day?'

'There may be some respite from heavy rain in the evening.'

'Lucy's tent is saturated. It won't take much more.'

'Ms Lucy is very welcome to stay at my house.'

'I want to sleep in the cave.'

'The cave is dry and sheltered from the wind.'

'But can you cook in there? We're both invited to dinner after the fireworks.'

'You can light a stove, or a fire in the cave mouth, where the smoke is drawn up and out.'

I take them to the steps and show them the narrow fissure in the rock. It comes from the cave and then cuts back under the cliff to blow clear. In this way you would hardly notice any smoke against the rock, and it is dispersed. So, Mr David must go into the cave to find the vent inside.

'There's driftwood tucked away in there, gnarled old drift-wood. Someone must have gathered it.'

'Not me. I never noticed it, or the smoke hole. Anyway, that's dinner organised at least.'

'And a wee bonfire besides. Only ten or so hours away, God help us.'

'You will come, won't you, Donald, when the beacons are lit.'

'I would be honoured.'

'And you'll bring the peats. About eight o'clock when the tide is going out.'

'We'll need to have a ceilidh, a storytelling round the fire.'

'About eight o'clock. I could not be forgetting the occasion. A story from the woman of the house, and one from each of the guests until dawn.'

I leave them to their work. There is something catching in their excitement, and I shall play my part. Tomorrow the storm may carry everything away in its fury.

The chimney cries, weeps. Wind k... keen-ing. Dark peat, cannot be morning.

Hold warm cup. Touch lips wet. She here, wool, wet.

Hair snow.

I once, cannot know.

Talks, talks.

She will... go. She knows, saw before. I saw. Must into weather, wild.

Child in creel. Seal suck. Her, in her... hold-ing.

Alright. Alright, rock bye-ing. Not cry.

Seal sing, weep to me, cry my...

Weep chimney, weep... all morning now, to go.

Brid... Bride... ie... Brid... *Ochon*, don't, not crying.

Who... she seal carry... hold. Not him going, in her... h-arms. Not cry. Going soon... in her... my skin.

Yes. In the wee shower, beneath that nozzle, with a spray of water coming out. Can't feel a thing. The skin beneath that water belongs to another body.

I'm Ice Man. It's not the cold of first impact I'm cold with. Long penetrating deep cold from wet and wind and dripping rocks, hour after hour. Till arm and hand follow one another in slow motion out of mind. But I'm still here, body, I'm going to come back to you.

Job done, man, job done. Imagine it – three beacons and a cairn with these scraped claws. Feel that warmth beginning to come through. I deserve this, I do.

Tried to persuade Lucy to come up here to shower and dry up. But no way. Told her we could cook and eat here too. Everything's tucked into that cave and she's off to shop, and use the shower at Donald's. She's adamant that cave's the venue.

Last night on shore, together.

According to himself, we can light a fire at the mouth and the smoke goes up that old vent. Time will tell, Donald, time will tell. Like that warm sensation, heat soothing through. God be thanked, whoever you might be, accept my humble thanks.

Maybe we could call them the McArthur Beacons. Those basins at the top are works of art, without a smidgin of doubt. But the wee drainage channel, that's a touch of genius, though I say it myself, which so far is the situation. There's design yes, but then there's engineering, construction. Haven't done anything like that for years, up at Granda's place, mending his tumbledown dykes. You never lose a skill like that, however far back. Like the women scooping up brush and dry branches and balancing them in one easy movement on their heads.

Just as well we've got that driftwood, though we're going to need the homebrew firelighters. Lucy will top herself if we can't get those things lit. But me and the Donald are a team. Couldn't happen anywhere besides here. That heat is inside now. Need to watch, not overheat my excited wee skull. Fry my brains.

Which makes you think... but no. I don't require a wee interim fry-up. What I do need soon, is a large mug of tea, plenty of milk and four sugars, dissolving as I start to sup. Alright, and maybe an egg roll or two. Tide me over till the dinner event. Definitely feeling more myself, better even. Couple of hours by the fire. Drink warm in the hand.

Not nodding off though. Listen to that wind; it's not giving up. Get out again – no point in sitting here on weather watch. Unfinished business of my own if it's nearly leaving time.

The causie's wet but not awash. Must be an angle to it draining downhill. Like everything else here, built to a purpose. Same with the path. You expect it to be squeegie after the downpour, but it's so rocky high on the ridge, rain runs off. You feel the wind up here, buffets that knock me off course but leave me standing. I'm well insulated with the spare jacket, two jerseys below and an old pair of waterproof breeks I found in the cupboard. Relic of some fishing trip and just the dab.

There's still rain driving in over the bay, but the clouds are starting to break up, re-mass, part again. The only thing visible beyond Eilean na Cleirich is churning sea.

Heavier underfoot as you come into the tree cover. Thank God for wellies. Mind the big puddles and whipping branches. When suddenly I'm through, out on the other side. Lea of the ridge; wind drops away. You can see why they built the village here. Why Abba put his church inland over the brow.

Everything deserted now in the wet. Over the wall carefully – no more scrapes – and lift the latch. Close the door behind me and listen to the silence flow back. Rain, wind, all outside these tight-fitting stones. Like a tomb or deep well shaft.

Place my feet firmly, quietly, on the flagstones. Not a sound. You would hardly know I was here. No-one knows. Pass the MacArthur memorial - *Fidei et Opera*. What kind of faith, what sort of works did they have in mind? The crest has a wreath of wild thyme and through it a sword. You can shove that back in the stone, or the loch, now boys. It's all done and by with.

There is definitely no-one else here. Sit on one of the wooden benches at the front. Everything looks towards the cross. It's so big, out of proportion to the church space. It belongs out in the landscape; but brought in here to save it from days like this. Stone-eating wind and wet. Need to preserve the carvings – those are artist works, not just mason tools.

Those guys weren't the gaffers though. Someone wanted it made and raised up looking out over the loch and down towards the headland. Not Abba, later, Donald said. Some high chief, head-bummer, bishop or whatever. This is my totem, my status symbol, my claim. By this sign, I hold the land, the people's labour, their souls and bodies. Is that too strong? Maybe it was a sign of peace, a waymark even for boats, to guide and bless. Maybe it was both things at the same time.

Not all the carvings are peaceful. Wild beasts with warriors or hunters. Gaping jaws of a lion, wild boar's tusks. Is that Daniel in his den? Saints and angels are near the top, out of the ruck. Then there's a few wee monks, mixing it with the earthlings, brute and human. They have their staffs in hand, and on their shoulders leather satchels for their bibles, pens and brushes. Maybe cheese and bread for their midday piece. No fried boar for these boys. Jesus mild and veggie.

Who knows, some of them might have been warriors too, soldiers of Christ or at least the abbot. Hardy if you think of all that travelling. African deserts to northern wastes of sea, like Abba. Ireland, Scotland, and further north to ice and fire. Till the Vikings came down on them brandishing both. The cross didn't protect them then, just guided in the destroyers.

Wheel and arms; sun and tree; circle and cross. Does it contain all the violence or channel it? Does a cross end blood feud or just name the price of settlement?

I didn't expect to be telling Lucy about Martin. Felt strange after thirty years, more than. I was back running from the Diamond, bodies crumpled. I could have lifted him up and carried him away in my arms. I wanted to mend him, close the wounds. If faith could make a difference, I believed – for that moment I had belief.

That's the trouble with stone. We're missing the man on that cross. A broken body taken down, cradled in his mother's arms.

If love could give life. No price to pay, no other claim or status. Just accepting the love. I miss you. You could be in my arms still.

He's left all their anger and violence behind. At peace; he wants me to be there as well.

Need a hankie. Man weeping in empty church.

Seems to be getting dimmer in here though. Tension of the day ebbing away. Quite warm, hugging myself with all these layers. Hands tucked into my armpits, could sit for a wee while and rest.

I am coming home. To my own body. Head first, the shoulders, breasts, belly, bum. Only then can I stretch out my arms, hands, legs, feet, under the hot stream. Letting the blood back in, gently.

Everything in and on me is wet. That is my element. Cold wet, warming wet, streaming rinsing wet. Blinded, submerged like people of the sea. I hardly need to come up for air.

Breathing out though, deep and long. All tension, effort washed away. It's done. The job is done, ready for a final showing. Imagine. After days, weeks, complete.

Just the ceremony tonight, our last celebration. Beacons ready to fire, all being well, but my part is done. Painting and sketches, packed, watertight. One video to capture the final event. Maybe one last big canvas in retrospect, a video installation perhaps, for the exhibition. That's for another day; tonight is the night. Only the weather can stop me now, but it won't. I'm too warm and strong to be defeated now.

Towel down. Lovely soft towels for such an austere man. Must be Bridget's hand here still. Need to rub and generate some friction in the damp steam. It's very kind to give me this hospitality. I would have perished without this respite, dissolved and washed out to sea. Yet the cave is amazingly dry and sheltered, far into the rock. I'll be safe there for tonight, like a solitary dragon guarding her treasures.

The bliss of dry clothes on my skin.

There are strange noises today from behind Bridget's closed door. The seal pup must be growing out of his basket. I go and fetch my coffee cup from the kitchen but there is no invitation to the back room.

'She is a bit unsettled with the wind.'

'Sounds like the seal is restless too.'

'It will have to go back to the sea.'

'Will Bridget be upset?'

'It must fish for itself or perish.'

I took a thick old-fashioned oatcake, with watery cream cheese, the flavour surprisingly pungent. Then another with honey.

Food for a goddess.

'What will be the best time to light the beacons?'

'Sometimes in the early evening before darkness, the wind calms for a time. Then the tide should be about right. I shall bring the peats and paraffin. When the flame catches, they will go up before they can become soaked through.'

'Will it be a good blaze?'

'Indeed, Lucy, the flames will not last long but there will be a fine fire. Beacons seen by friend and stranger.'

'Fantastic. You've certainly been a friend, Donald. It couldn't happen without you. You must stay later and have something to eat.'

'You and Mr David must come here where a meal can be cooked.'

'Thank you, Donald, but I'm going to have my last night in the cave. It is the women's refuge after all. I can cook there.'

'As you choose.'

'Perhaps you could bring some –'

'*Uisge bheatha.*'

'Well, yes, some whisky will be very welcome, but I was going to say, a story.'

'For the ceilidh. I shall be honoured to come to your ceilidh, Ms Lucy, especially on this night.'

'Excellent, so my next job has to be getting along to the shop. Otherwise, the hospitality will be very poor, and I'll be shamed.'

Wet grasses on old stones, she bathes her feet walking carefully across the ruins. Shawled, stooped against the wind, she moves effortlessly to the doorway. Lifts latch and enters. The door clicks softly back in place.

Man on bench bowed beneath the cross. Hands held beneath his arms like Columba's plants. Eyes are closed in sleep, tears dried upon his face.

One palm on brow, one on shoulder, paused in silence. Breath of spirit.

Her eyes are open, deep blue in brown creased face. Lines of sorrow and of gladness.

Gentle touch, withdrawn, she moves away.

Trudged back along the shore, bulging bag in each hand, I feel no let-up in wind or rain. Angry waves are breaking round the beacons, and a crepuscular gloom seems to be closing in on the beach.

The little stove sputters into life, giving my cave mouth a glow against the gathering dark. Thankfully I had a spare bottle of gas. Get everything unpacked.

No time for finesse here though, even if I ever had such a thing, in the kitchen anyway. Dollops of oil, halved onions, whole garlic cloves. When that sizzles, dump in chicken pieces, then sausages, and finally some pieces of bacon, curled up. Declined the frozen steak, in case it wasn't for frying. I don't really understand meat. The other pot will do for potatoes. 'Spuds' in Dave-speak.

With all that cooking, I can spread out the blankets and pillows for seating. Then everything will be aired and warm for sleeping in the back later. The hostess shall not be put to shame.

Mind you, what about this ceilidh I've announced? A story from the man or the woman of the house, according to Donald. Woman of the house? So that's me or Bridget. She can barely speak, or doesn't want to speak, and I don't know any stories, not like that anyway. A woman with no story to tell. To be fair, my mind's been on other things.

Well, I'll just have to give way to the guests. I'm not really the host anyway, not compared to Donald. He is the keeper of the stories here. And I've invited him to my refuge, so he should have first place at the ceilidh. I will focus on the art-works, and yes, Dave, on the food.

Suddenly awake, staring in the face of my electronic clock. Seven. I fell asleep by the fire. Right out. How did I get back from the church? Barely remember. Self-propelled after dozing. I'm still in zombie time from manual labour – weeks, months, years run off me like rain.

Need to get going or I'll miss the big event. Muffle up in all the layers and down to the beach. Light's very dim but it feels as if the rain's slackened off. Clouds still sweeping in and nothing to be seen beyond the island.

'You've decided to join us.'

'Sorry, fell asleep. Came over all relaxed somehow.'

'Exhaustion after hard labour.'

'Grafted as never before. I see Donald's done his stuff though.'

Waves still lapping hungrily round the beacons, but the tops are happed over with plastic covers, firmly tied round the girth. Old fertiliser bags likely, with the peats snug and dry below.

'Where is he?'

'Building a fire in the cave mouth. He swears the smoke will go up the hole whatever wind blows.'

Sure enough, the tall figure stoops over his fire, dressed head to toe in tight-fitting waterproofs. He looks up towards me and nods.

'So, what's the schedule?'

'Half an hour at the most, and then the lights go on. We all begin together at the middle beacon, and then you and Donald go to the outriders, one in each direction.'

'And you?'

'I have to get a close up of the first blaze, but then I'll move towards the cairn to pan the shoreline and get all three fires in one shot. I'm going to film as long as they burn.

'As long as they do burn.'

'It can't go wrong now, Dave.'

'Yes, mam.'

'Then we eat and ceilidh, in the local manner.'

'Now that sounds good. Here's some liquid offerings.'

'Thanks. Come up now and pull the first corks. I'm putting you in charge of the drinks.'

'We get to start now!'

'If only to keep warm. Oh, and I'm giving you a camera for stills. Just to catch some different angles after the beacons are all lit. But not before.'

'No problem.'

'Come on then, go to it.'

Like being in the boy scouts. Forgot to salute.

'Evening, Donald.'

He's intent on his fire, and truth be told it is a work of art. Bleached, gnarled driftwood has been woven round like an upside-down basket. Round the whole is a containing ring of stones. Somewhere in the middle dry kindling has already caught. You can see the flicker on his lean face. Maybe a smouldering of peats too, all designed to set the old, compacted timber burning.

Behind the fire, further in, two big pots are simmering on Lucy's stove. As you go through it's still raining at your back, but then the air is wholly windless. One pot's full of spuds, the other's savoury. That's my girl; I knew she wouldn't let me down.

We're deep in here underneath the ledge of rock that divides beach from scrubland slopes. The cave then takes a sharp right turn; it's darker but more spacious. I can just make out Lucy's tent strung up to dry, and all her possession stacked round against the walls.

'Will you be alright in here?'

'Of course, look what I found.'

She shines her torch on the roof. High up where the cave roof twists into its inner throat, a circle is incised in the stone and within it a cross. But I'm not allowed to stand and gaze. Back to the reception suite, where I'm handed the corkscrew. Never seen Lucy so high – outgoing, confident, yet brittle with it.

What if it goes wrong after the huge build-up? But Donald seems satisfied with his pyrotechnics. At least I'm not on that front line, except in a subaltern role. He's pulling off the waterproof breeks now, revealing a sporran, silver kilt pin. That'll be the hunting MacLean. And look at yours truly; talk about dressing up.

Donald accepts my proffered glass a little quizzically, but with good grace. Bubblie's not his tipple.

Lucy raises a toast, 'To the beacons!'

Aware of some other woman writing up my journal. She is acutely conscious of me gesticulating, toasting, chattering like an incipient hysteric. And she realises how tense I have been through this whole time in Scotland, hanging in with a grim determination to carry it through.

If for one moment I had flagged, lost concentration, given in to discomfort, doubted my own will to deliver, I would have been lost. Now I can see the tension outside myself, objectified. That is not me, or else I am it. Fortunately, it doesn't matter any longer. The outcome is in Donald MacLean's hands now, not mine. This is his place.

He has prepared the firing like a military operation, with Dave enlisted as staff sergeant, his right-hand man. Has to be a man of course. My role is to watch and wait, a mere spectator. But what they don't understand is that someone else will have the last word, as observer and recorder. It's that other woman who will define what happened.

Everything is dark grey outside, but the rain is no longer horizontal. I pick up my old stills camera and the video, positioning myself beside the cairn. Donald and David are at the central beacon, one each side, knives in hand. In his other Donald has a lighter. How can one tiny flame ignite this sequence?

For a moment I foretaste humiliation, a spasm of nausea. Everything is on pause. How ridiculous can she get?

Neither man shows any hint of my surreal expectations. Standing intently, watching as the tide creeps back. Then they look at each other.

'Ready?'

'Ready.'

Is that my high-pitched voice?

Both knives in one swift cut. Dave pulls off the cover. A spark. Light catches. Flames rise round a black core.

The lens reflects every flicker, red blue flowering of the peat. 'Now!'

I sense them splitting each way along the shore. But my eye is tight around the basin, snapping in sequence as the blue blacks and turns to red gold.

Back to video as the other covers go off. Quickly the red blue takes. Dave must have had a lighter too. Switching from one side to the other. I see a wave breaking on one beacon, foam round his legs, trying to reclaim the outposts. But the flames are unstoppable, blazing out along the beach.

Panning, I catch tongues of fire leaping into the darkness. Someone's shouting. Can't listen. Shifts now this way and that, overview, close up. Pillars of flame almost lighting up the bay. Must get that angle out over the water. The whole bay – is that the island?

Fire, air, water. Can't see the men now.

Look, it's working. The whole thing, my design. God, it's working! No more pics, just look. Weeks of grind blaze out in glory.

'Magic!'

'I've got them.'

Even as the words are spoken, those unquenchable fires begin to weaken, dwindle back into their basins. We all stand watching as the blaze subsides into a flickering glow, as if someone had covered them again without extinguishing their light.

'They have burnt well despite the damp.'

'Well? Donald, you're a genius. It was spectacular.'

'The way it has been for you.'

'Quick, let me get your picture before the fire's out. Donald, Dave, you too, beside the cairn, light at the back.'

I realise suddenly how wet the lens is in this rain. The camera's crying. Or is it my tears, joy. Lucy's mark, recorded in nature. Not to be lost or forgotten.

They look so proud of themselves in their crazy hats. Captured in time.

'I thank you, Lucy, for your fine meal. And now I would like to pour each one of you another dram.'

'Here's the bottle.'

'We have toasted the occasion with that named whisky, David, and it was very acceptable. But I would like you now to taste this local whisky, which has no name.'

He reaches into his jacket and comes out with a square shaped bottle. The liquid glints in the firelight as he draws an old stopper and pours each one of us a generous measure.

'I have kept this bottle for many years, but now there is no reason to keep it any longer. *Slàinte*.'

Smooth, smoky. The smallest sip filling with warmth. Dip into the bottom of the well.

'That's the spirit, right enough.'

'Every muscle in my body just breathed out. Should we have our stories now?'

'Stories?'

'Don't play dumb, Dave, you know this is a ceilidh.'

'Ah, how could I forget? The woman of the house will tell the first story. Isn't that the way of it, Donald?'

'No. You've already seen my story tonight out there on the beach. I've nothing else in me to tell. Donald, please, you must have first place, because we are truly guests of your tradition, this place.

He nods gravely towards her as if acknowledging a great courtesy.

'Well, if you wish, I shall recite an old tradition of the place. And if as I tell it, there is some confusion with my own memories of the sea, then that may not be a bad thing, as every tale should be clothed anew in the garments of the time and of the storyteller.'

Whisky is not preventing the flow. Resting in the palm of his hand, even the storm has drawn back to listen.

'As young seamen we used to ride the currents up the Sound of Jura. I was telling Ms Lucy this when she walked out to Eilean na Cleirich. We took our chances on the lip of the whirlpool of Corryveckan, which lies between Jura and the Island of Scarba.

'Long ago, before Abba and the white monks came to this land, a priest of the old religion lived on Scarba. His name was Dubhthas and he was known and respected in all of Ireland and Scotland because of the great power of the pool. And on the island there were also living a fellowship of druids, and a community of women dedicated to the goddess who ruled over everything. In accordance with a cycle of ancient times and seasons, Dubhthas and his people would climb the cliffs at the south end of Scarba to watch the fearful opening of the whirlpool, and make sacrifice to the goddess.

'Now amongst the maidens dedicated to the goddess were nine women of especial beauty, later called the women of Jura, renowned in story and song. But they were set apart, reserved to the sacred mother who alone could confer her favours. And many young men came to Scarba from near and far, to face whatever trials were decreed and see if they might be chosen.

'And there was a young chief named Breacan, who came from the far north where rumour of the great pool of Scarba had travelled. And he wanted to see for himself and pay his respects to Dubhthas. Breacan was a proud sea-going warrior, a tower of a man, famed for strength and beauty. And he was not pledged to any woman, though many had set their hearts on him.

'He came here by ship and sailed in a small boat to Scarba. There he saw and lost his heart to one of the nine maidens. The story says that she was raven haired with skin as white as milk and smooth as a river pearl. Yet she was modest and retiring in obedience to her vow, and it was by chance that as Breacan came past the veil slipped to reveal her lovely features. As she turned to catch the veil, she saw the most beautiful man her eyes had ever beheld, and their gaze met.

'Being a man without deceit, Breacan went to Dubhthas and asked for the love of the raven-haired maiden. Dubhthas was disturbed by this request since he liked the young chief and desired friendship with the men of the north. Nonetheless he had no choice other than to set a trial by death for the young hero. And this was the test. That Breacan should anchor his birlinn, his galley, at the centre of the whirlpool, within sight of Scarba, on three successive tides.

'Breacan returned to his ship to brood on these chances. The crew urged him to weigh anchor and return home. Instead, Breacan ordered three new anchor cables to be prepared. The first was made of the finest wool spun and plaited, then plaited and plaited once more. The second was made in the same way but of horsehair from the tails of horses. And the third was plaited, then plaited, and plaited once more from the hair of maidens. So, the cables were complete.

'As the time for the testing drew near, Breacan sailed from the sea loch on a southerly breeze. But as soon as he came into open waters the wind died, becalming him and his crew. They put out the oars but suddenly a thick mist descended, and they were unable to continue for fear of running onto the rocks. They sat in a miserable cloud, brooding over their captain's fate.

'On the third day, the wind freshened, fog lifted, and at Breacan's insistence they sailed on for Scarba. But as they approached the island, they saw it ringed by galleys. Word had gone out near and far and many had travelled to witness the young chief's ordeal. That night there was feasting, music and story, such as was never seen before on that island and has never been seen since.'

He leans in towards the fire, as if drawing on its energy to continue. His hand brushes back a lock of white springing hair from his brow, clearing an inner eye.

'The day of reckoning dawned. The sea seemed flat and calm with no wind of which you might speak. Breacan sailed his galley into the slack where the whirlpool would break. His crew laid out three anchors and he ordered the cable of wool tied to one, of horsehair to the second, and the cable wound from maiden hair to the third. They were all cast.

'And they settled down to wait upon events. Beside Breacan sat his hunting hound, Luath, who loved him beyond all living things. Above, the shores of Scarba and of Jura were crowded with onlookers, while a throng of galleys rode at anchor beyond reach of the current.

'As the tide began to run the whirlpool stirred into life. The water revolved slowly at first, but then quickened pace, whipping up a wind. The galley dipped into the corrie, the hollow at the heart of the pool, and was almost lost to sight amidst a churning of foam. The three anchor cables stretched and strained, but all three held. When without warning the horsehair cable broke in an explosive crack.

'The sailors were terrified, but Breacan swore by the loyalty of Luath that the remaining two cables would hold the ship safe. The water smoothed, the sun set, and they hunkered down to await the next tide. There was no feasting that night, and no music. Everyone stayed at their stations.

'Darkness lay on sea and land when the crew felt their boat tremble. Both anchor cables tightened, creaked and stretched as the galley was sucked down by the gathering force. It was so black that none from sea or shore could see what was happening. This time the sea raced harder, the winds blew fiercer, but the cables held fast. When, with an explosive crack, the cable wound from the finest wool broke. The sound reverberated against the cliffs. The ship lurched, violently spinning round on the one remaining anchor, but its cable held.

'Morning lightened, but the sun did not appear. Grey clouds scudded overhead, and rain-filled squalls swept in between the islands. The lowered sails of the galley flapped wearily. The crew were sure their end had come. But Breacan swore by the loyalty of Luath, who loved him beyond any living creature, that they could place undying trust in the hair given by the Scarba maiden. But when the third tide came the whirlpool broke into itself with treble fury, and the cable snapped with an explosive crack.

'The spectators gazed in horror as the doomed ship was dragged inexorably under, and every other galley on the outer ring went down with it into blackness. As the last current subsided the face of the sea was shrouded in terrible silence. Everyone stared into the emptiness. Then silence was broken by a heartrending cry and the maiden of Scarba, whom Breacan had loved beyond all living things, cast herself from the cliff into the last ripple of the pool.'

Eyes narrow into small black points, as if he too had been sucked into that dark.

'It was said afterwards that a woman whom Breacan slighted had inserted a hair into the rope in order to avenge herself on the lover by whom she had been jilted. But perhaps it was already fated, since none before or since has overcome the whirlpool of Corryvreckan. She had once more exacted a toll in human lives. Against that inexorable power the deepest love was helpless.

'Three days later Breacan's body was washed ashore on Jura, and entangled in his limbs was the body of faithful Luath. They are buried together now on Cruachan at the north end of Scarba, looking down on the maiden's watery grave. Her mortal remains were never found, yet people say that the whirlpool still carries the name of her lover.'

Crackle of driftwood. Far beat of waves on the shore.

We are looking into the fire rather than at each other.

'That's some story, Donald. I think I'll need another dram.'

So, we all receive another glass of whisky from the golden bottle.'

'I'm going to have some water with this.'

'The spring water is best.'

Imbued with the scent of brown earth it bubbles into its stone basin, undisturbed by wild weather.

'Water and spirit, as the women of the house would say.'

'Indeed. *Slàinte.*'

'Thank you for that story, Donald. It was a sad one, and I only wish the lovely woman of Scarba could have a name.'

'The tradition has not kept her name, if it was once known.'

'The nameless one. That way she keeps coming back at you.'

'You sound as if you have met her, David.'

'No, I don't think so. Though I did have a strange dream at the church today.'

'You went back.'

'Do you remember that woman you saw on the beach, Lucy, with the shawl, carrying a seal.'

'Sometimes I think I dreamt her.'

'Well, I think it was her, an old lady, very kind and gentle. This dream seemed to lift a gloom from me, some burden.'

'There is a woman who walks on the shore sometimes. They call her the grey lady.'

'Have you seen her, Donald?'

'No, but Bridget has, many times in the past.'

'Who is she?'

'No-one knows, but some say she was one of the women who lived at the Well House, in Abba's time.'

'My God, I've seen a ghost.'

'Why is she still here?'

'No-one knows.'

'She seems a positive spirit anyway.'

'A blessing, not a curse.'

'To each who blesses, a blessing, and to each who curses...'

'Are you ok, Donald?'

'Fine, just a little tired.'

'Perhaps we should wrap up now and head home?'

'No way, we're still to have your story.'

'Indeed, there must be another tale.'

'Then I'll make some coffee.'

'Alright, though I wasn't brought up with this ceilidh business. But I did go to Donegal on holidays, and they were always telling stories. It was like going to a magic place for me, out of the city, and what came back to me thinking about tonight was a memory not a traditional story, if you'll forgive a personal angle. It is about seals.'

'I think I like the sound of this.'

'It is yourself, David, that must be choosing the story to tell. For then it will be the right tale.'

'Well, there was a big bay there too, near my Granda's cottage, with lots of rocky inlets. And there's an island out in the bay mouth – Gola they call it. I was always down in that bay, scrabbling amidst the sand and rocks. No change there. Then there was driftwood, old floats, nets, shells, and other plastic rubbish, all for the taking.

'Granda had a wee shed above the beach. His clobber was stashed in there – tar, timber, paint, nets, fish boxes. It was a smelly old bothy but dry and snug on a wet day.

'So, one time the rain came in, dreich and grey. I was getting cold on the beach, and I took shelter in the shed, pluitering amongst nets and boxes. I must have settled down there in the lumber and fallen asleep. That's a talent of mine to this day, even in dangerous places, I can just snooze off. Must be in the genes. My excuse anyroads.

'Couple of hours later this wee fella came to. And it hit me right between the eyes, or nostrils. Foul, rotten fish smell, overpowering. Before I could react, get moving, it was on me, thrashing, squealing. Thwack, and another thwack it dished out. The poor craitur was in terror – the shed was its hidey-hole. And I was screaming blue murder. The oily pelt of it was on my skin. Tangled in fear.

'Some instinct came to my rescue. I scrambled up and got out the door. Then I ran.

'When I came back with Granda he had a gun. But the seal was gone. I'm sure the seal, he or she, meant me no harm. But I've been nervous around them ever since. Seems a bit stupid repeating it round here, given recent events, but imagine a seal trying to get into your bed.'

'Yes, exactly like me on the island. I was asleep and the seal didn't realise I was there.'

'Seals can smell, Lucy. Perhaps sometimes they come looking for human company. Curious at any rate.'

'That's a strange idea.'

'What?'

'They like our smell.'

'Yours anyway.'

'Talking about smells, who would like coffee? I've got some real brew bubbling away here.'

'Coffee? After hotpot, fruit pie and cheese. You'll make a brilliant wee wife one day.'

'That's enough from you. The so-called hotpot was stir fry, and the fruit pie came from Glasgow. Of course, I did make the cheese with a deer's milk from the hill.'

'It was a grand feed, was it not, Donald.'

'A fine meal, David, indeed.'

'And cooked at a cave mouth in a gale. The ancestors would be fair bursting with pride.'

'Here's your coffee. How come you're so cheerful tonight?'

'Lousing time, Lucy, job done, as instructed. But, in truth, some kind of cloud lifted today, even as the black ones were rolling in.'

'That's good.'

'Coffee, Donald?'

'Thank you. Will you have another dram, David?'

'One for the road.'

'Indeed. If Ms Lucy does not have another story for us.'

'I could not compete, believe me. Anyway, my head is swimming.'

'The woman with no story to tell.'

'Tomorrow is another day.'

'Thank you, Donald, well put.'

'*Slàinte!*'

'*Slàinte, agus beannachd leibh.*'

The ceilidh is complete. The fire must be banked up to keep some warmth and light through the hours of darkness. It will protect the place of sleep. I pour one final dram on the embers.

Mr David should be guided up the steps and steered in the right direction. He is beyond himself now, but strangely at peace after the troubles of his mind. I envy him that lightness of step, however unsteady. He will reach home before the last gale breaks.

The woman of the house is pale and drained of strength. Her work here is finished with the firing of the beacons. She should sleep well also.

I shall walk the shore, till my own mind settles. Night watching. The storm withdrew only to soon return in fury. Every living creature has gone to ground, every plant lies low. Only man in his foolishness attempts to stand upright in the face of nature.

Nothing remains on the beach. A great blackness has settled in the bay waiting to cover the earth. I shall give myself up to the keeping of the elements and bide the outcome. There is none left to gather me if I am broken. But I shall put myself at defiance and walk the whirlpool's edge.

There were three fires burning on the shore tonight, but they have been doused. Why put out the lights when the worst is to come? Yet he is still watching.

I see a lowering blackness on the ocean, and far out I see a boat riding on the storm. The frame dips and soars with the waves, like a gannet. The crash and roar of sea tries to drown its spirit. But the frail vessel skims through the spray, round the howling mouth that would devour it.

Come home. My arms cry out.

God save us, from the time of dread and testing.

Eye of the storm, out in the western sea, the curragh's back has broken. It is engulfed down into the deep.

When from the swirl beneath, a sleek black form, charge of living flesh, rises and lifts the mortal frame, arms wrapped round, rising, swimming to the light. Hold fast, wave diver, sea courser.

Where is their landfall? Through this gloom, massing on the water's face. Homecoming to these outstretched rocks, even broken, lifeless. Do not abide treacherous times. I cannot wait forever.

In that at least we are alike, Bridie's bodach and I. Yet I shall outlast.

Pulling, clawing up towards the surface. Like a drowning man. Thumps of wind on the roof. Banging head. Cries. Stumbling through I have to shove the door open with my shoulder.

'God, Lucy.'

'Dave, Dave, sorry – please.'

I pull her inside and ram the door shut.

'Thank God, you're here. I thought you'd gone.'

'Christ, what's wrong, Lucy? You're alright. I was just sleeping.'

'You're here, I thought you'd left.'

She's dripping wet. Get the fire on. Fetch blanket. She folds into the chair, lets me pull off her sodden jacket. Crumpled night clothes wrapped round warm and tight. Stop the shivering. Kneel and hold her till sobs subside.

'You're safe. In the Well House.'

'I thought... it was...'

'Don't, don't speak. Wait there and I'll get us some tea.'

Back to the room. Pull on trousers, jersey, shoes without socks. Then out to the hob. Dazed but acting clearly. Kettle, water, mugs. Two strong teas with sugar and a splash of whisky. Wind rattling round me like the house is at sea. It's cold.

She's staring into the gas.

'Here, take this.'

'Tea.'

'It's hot.'

She sips gingerly. Now I see the bloody feet. Cut on the rocks. I pour the rest of the kettle into a basin with more water from the tap. Bathing gently as she sups her tea. Empty the basin. Kettle on again. This time I leave the feet to soak. They must be smarting, but she barely seems aware.

We're sitting each side of the fire. Nothing said. Just listening to the scream of the wind, and rain like shrapnel on the windows.

'Better?'

She nods.

'Can you talk?'

Another nod.

'No rush.'

'Dave, it was so strange. I feel a fraud. It was only afterwards that I panicked.'

Say nothing. Let it come in her own good time.

'I woke up, and there was something, someone in the cave beside me. Right at the back. I could hear the wind howl outside, but it was quiet in. And that smell.'

'Seal?'

'Pressing against me, warm and fetid.'

'Did it attack you?'

'No, and that's the strangest bit. I wasn't afraid. He wasn't afraid. I reached out and stroked the flank. And... this is going to sound crazy.'

'Go on, I'm listening.'

'The skin was rough and bristly but then my fingers found the scar, puckered tissue, hard to the touch. It was the bull, Dave.'

'He'd come visiting again, Lucy. He had your scent.'

'He just lay there for a while. I left my hand on his old wound. I don't know how long. Then he backed away and I could hear him on the stone floor.'

'Out and away.'

'I think so, it was dead quiet in the dark. Then I panicked, scrambled out and ran. I don't know why, I was fine.'

'Just the shock of it.'

'I wasn't afraid, Dave, not of the bull. He was looking for some kind of comfort. Or even – but this is the madwoman bit.'

'What?'

'He was trying to give comfort, some kind of reassurance.'

'To you.'

'Perhaps, or to whoever was in the cave, taking refuge from the storm.'

'He may have got the wrong woman.'

'I hope not, I hope whatever brought him went away soothed.'

'Didn't soothe your feet though.'

'It was so stupid, running like that. My feet feel much better.'

'Could you sleep?'

'I think so.'

'We'll tuck you up through by. I'll sleep at the fire.'

'Listen, Dave, I don't want –'

'No trouble, and we'll leave the door ajar, let some light through.'

'Sleep beside me, Dave. I don't want to be alone.'

I take her through and settle her down, well wrapped up. Then I lie down beside her, and she snuggles in, subsiding soon into sleep. Breathing easily, her mind at rest in some untroubled place.

Was it a nightmare? Didn't like to suggest that when her recall was so vivid. Some memory of the old seal on the island, revived by the storm. My fault for retelling that story.

Maybe he did come up the beach though, looking for shelter. Maybe he knew his way to that cave and didn't expect to find it occupied. Bit like Granda's wee shed. If it was a nightmare she'd have been terrified there and then, not later. What else could it have been if not a seal?

Lay there beside sleeping beauty for a restless couple of hours. Then eased myself out without waking her. Pulled the bedroom door to. Brewed up some fresh tea ready for morning. Storm calming at last. Almost six-thirty.

Phoned Donald MacLean. He's an early bird.

'MacLean here.'

'It's David at Well Croft, Donald. Sorry to disturb you so early but there's been a spot of trouble overnight.'

'Is the chimney down?'

'No, nothing like that. It's Lucy. Something came into the cave and scared her witless. She came running up here and made a real mess of her feet on the rocks.'

'Do you need the doctor?'

'I don't think so. She's still sleeping but I'll ask her when she wakes up.'

'Was it a seal?'

'She thinks so. What else could it have been?'

'That old bull is still hiding on Eilean na Cleirich. He might have come ashore for shelter, the night that was in it. The submarines sometimes put a boat onto the beach. Not likely though in this weather unless they saw the fire. Was it large?'

'I think so. Do you want to me to go down to the cave?'

'No, stay where you are. I will deal with it.'

The line goes dead; he's rung off.

Oilskins and boots are still at the door from last night. I have the shotgun with a box of cartridges. What did that filthy creature want in the cave? The time has come to rid us of the vermin.

The gale is weakening but I must still push my door against the wind. Coming down onto the bay I am buffeted back and forwards. Rain is coming off the sea like storm spray. I put my head down and walk into the weather.

It is a terrible thing for such a woman to be affronted, assaulted in this way. She has come in search of peace for her painting, but her sanctuary has been violated by a brute beast. It is not to be borne.

The first and third beacons have broken in the storm. Much pleasure the night fires gave for their time, but now the sea reclaims them. Only the cairn will survive above the tide. I gauge my approach from those stones to the cave mouth. Without doubt these are his tracks dragging up the beach and then back down to the water. He has already gone back to sea, or the island.

The refuge is empty, apart from her bed clothes, the remains of last night, and her pictures stacked beyond. Nothing is disordered or destroyed. Is there a lingering odour? The ashes are sodden.

I should have stayed here through the violence of the night. It was my duty to insist. I should have known. But he shall not escape again.

Hurrying back along the beach I lift my latch for a second time. No sound from the backroom. I replace the shotgun and take my rifle. It is already loaded. I take a long breath and listen. Open the door. She is dozing in the warmth with the creature in its basket below. But as I lift and grip it under one arm, there are squeals. She wakes, moaning her refusal.

Out of the room. The pup squirms. Through the front door, pulling it behind, into the grey light. Along the beach again, not as far as the first beacon. There is no need. I throw the barking writhing thing into the waves.

He twists in the surf, and I club him with the rifle butt, driving him out. This will bring the bull within range. Another hit. They were right about that. The cub is fighting gamely but without help it will drown. Again, I strike and raise the gun.

My arm is caught, dragged back. I try to shake free but it clings sobbing with effort, moaning and grunting. With my free hand I hit back at the bundle. It falls away. I strike again, driving the butt down into a limp mess.

Where is the seal? Riding the first waves. I train the rifle and fire four times. Blood spurts. Where is the old bull when he sees his kind attacked? The bundle catches my eye, heaped with strange neatness in the tide, like rags for collection. I could turn them over with the long barrel of my gun.

The choice has been made. I throw my rifle out into the waves. Let the sea have them. I must leave, climbing up the steps onto the ridge, wind and rain at my back.

Past the Well House. 'Donald, did you see the seal?' 'Donald, what happened on the beach?' Always, the outsider brings trouble and danger. Why could you not let us in peace, McArthur, coming back like a cur to its vomit? Was one bloodletting not enough for you, Irish curse?

Through the wood, and past the chapel, it's cross hidden from view. Only the dark pillars can guide me now, towards the headland. Onto the salt road. Sharp and clean as a kill.

The door flaps and bangs. Lobby agape.

One half-eaten bowl of porridge on the table; tea standing cold.

In the hall his shotgun leans against a ransacked cupboard.

The backroom is empty, hearth unlit, a tumbled basket at its side.

Where is Brigid? What is the worst?

On the shore storm tide thrown debris - driftwood, tangled nets, floats. And a humped shape below high-water mark. Cast up.

What is the worst that has happened?

Bridie is lost to herself, beyond kenning. The knot is untied. She can journey now to the ends of the earth.

This worn pathway between chapel, Well House and the cave formed her known bounds. Now nothing binds her to this place, or to me. And I must be leaving, borne over waves and islands without landfall.

These feet are tender. What was I thinking of, running through that storm. Like some maenad. Head seems to be in one piece though. So far.

'Tea's on the table. No whisky this time.'

'Thanks, but the whisky worked. That's the deepest sleep I've had in weeks.'

'How are the feet?'

'Sore.'

'You can bathe them again and see if you need the doctor.'

'They'll be fine, just cuts and bruises. What was I thinking, running out of there in the middle of the night?'

'I phoned Donald MacLean. He's going along to check the cave. He thinks it was the big seal that was hanging about the island, come in for shelter. I don't blame you; it must have been terrifying.'

'Like your experience.'

'And that overpowering smell making you gag. Musty, fetid. I shouldn't have raked all that back up.'

Sipping at my hot tea, thinking about Dave's story.

'Strange thing is, though, it wasn't like that, like your experience.'

'What way?'

'I don't think I was afraid of him, or even surprised. I understood that he wanted company, some creature contact beyond the gale. It felt good, right, touching his wound. Does that make any sense? It was only after he had gone that I reacted. Over-reacted.'

'It was natural, Lucy, pure shock.'

'Maybe, but I think it was all the tensions of these last weeks, months, finally exploding.'

'So, you feel better?'

'I think so. Definitely – he was the trigger, not the cause. More release than terror.'

'Well, that's a relief; it felt a bit like fear last night, for me anyway.'

'Dave, I'm so sorry, but you were brilliant. I can't thank you enough. It's becoming addictive.'

'Any port in a storm.'

'No, this was the sanctuary I needed, like all those women who lived here long since.'

'My woman at the church, or the wee shawlie lady with the herbal cures.'

'She was no ghost. Those plants are real.'

'Right enough, armpit ready. So, what's the plan for today?'

'We need a dry spell so I can get packed up.'

'I think that rain's slackening, even while we've been sitting here, there's a difference in the way it's hitting the windows. When's Ian coming?'

'Late afternoon at the earliest, depending on the drive. We were planning to stay a night in Oban before heading home. If the worst comes to the worst, I'll just have to shove some of my clobber into the car wet.'

'I'll come down and give a hand.'

'There's no need, we'll manage.'

'But I want to meet Ian.'

'He's one of the good guys, despite everything I've put him through.'

'Job complete; family beckons.'

'Yes, Ian and his two kids. They are my family – it takes being away to realise that. So, when are you off, Dave?'

'Tomorrow, just to Glasgow for a medical. And then…'

'You're going back.'

'If they'll have me.'

'But you're ready.'

'Nothing else for it. I do feel better in myself. And that's not just down to the ghosts, Lucy.'

'We've helped each other. But, if I'm going to get down to that beach, I need to raid your wardrobe, Dave.'

'Is nothing sacred?'

Lean over and plant a kiss on his forehead.

'Alright, it's only a loan mind. And you've still to tend those feet.'

Clouds over the bay are breaking up. Splashes of light on white horses. The island is rising back from the sea. Morning was held back, but now it's a surge of sun and fresh breeze. Everything is given again regardless. That's the mystery.

Hobbling down in three pairs of socks stuffed into Dave's wellies. Sore but bearable. Doing the return trip.

Coming onto the rocky lip the beach is strewn with debris. The beacons have crumbled from the basins down, leaving their stumps as transient markers. Only the cairn has made it through the night. How can the sea erode all that stone? It's continual force remorseless. Have I caught any of that in my drawing, painting, construction, photomontage, video?

If I haven't done it here, then I'll not do it anywhere. Given the morning 'that is in it', as Donald would say, who cares?

No sign of him as I edge gingerly down the steps to the cave mouth. No signs of disturbance either, so I shuffle inside. Dim and still. Odourless. I stoop to the spring and put some water on my hand and brow. Cool and clean tasting as ever. How does the pool drain, always level, without overspill?

Enough. Spread the tent and bedclothes out at the mouth where they can air and dry. Weigh smaller things down with a picture. Nothing much more I can do till Ian arrives. Dave's coming down to help load up. The fetch-and-carry man; navvie by name. His voice is in my head now.

'Excuse me, madam.'

Two figures in uniform are looking down from the top of the steps. Surveying my demolished campsite.

'Morning.'

They come down.

'Sorry to disturb you. Have you been camping here?'

'Yes, I've been here for a few weeks. Lucy Salter, I'm an artist. I arranged it with Mr MacLean.'

'Donald MacLean?'

'Yes. Is there anything wrong?'

'This is PC Susan Gibb, I'm Sergeant Ross, from Lochgilphead Police Station. We're wondering if you saw anything unusual last night?'

'Well, it was a wild night. I had to move everything into the cave. Then something disturbed me, and I spent the rest of the night up at the Well House with Mr McArthur.'

'MacArthur?'

'Dave McArthur, he's staying there on leave.'

'Right. Can you say what disturbed you? Was it an intruder?'

'I think it was a seal.'

'It's late in the season for seals.'

'I saw it out on the island a few days back. Mr MacLean guided me out. Is there anything wrong?'

Sergeant Ross paused considering. Seagulls wheeled raucously, diving to plunder the wrack.

'Unfortunately, Ms Salter, a body was found on the beach early this morning by local fishermen.'

'That's terrible, was someone washed ashore?'

'There's been no formal identification, but it was an elderly female, well known locally.'

'Not Bridget MacLean?'

'Did you know Mrs MacLean?'

'I visited her a few times. She didn't seem fully aware. Maybe she got out of the house by accident. Poor Donald, he'll never forgive himself.'

A look was exchanged.

'When did you last see Mr MacLean?'

'He was here last night, having a meal with Dave, Dave McArthur, and myself. Where is he?'

'He appears to be missing.'

'Could he have been washed out trying to save Bridget?'

'We don't know. Do you think we would find Mr McArthur at Well Croft?'

'Yes, he's packing. Getting ready to leave today, like me.'

'Thank you, Miss, Ms Salter, you've been very helpful.'

'Please let me know what's happened, and if I can really help in any way. It's terrible.'

But their backs are already turned disappearing over the bank. Something is wrong, horribly wrong. I feel nausea rising and vomit into the sand.

Formal statement concluded. I'm allowed to leave but only by promising to stay at the Glasgow address until investigations are concluded.

It all depends on tides and currents, if another body will be washed ashore.

I was packing everything into the car, dry and damp – thank God for polybags – when the dog handler burst in.

His big Alsatian sniffed round the causie, then shot off in the direction of the headland.

Last seen round here, by a shepherd on the hill. More than an hour after I phoned, but not much more. Why didn't I even look outside? We were still cooped up from the storm chatting about last night. Did he look in, and then leave us to it?

Or he wasn't for stopping, either way.

Tip leftover stuff into the bin. Tidying up for an inspection, which won't come.

Need to get down to the beach. Lucy will be distressed about Donald and Mrs MacLean, Bridget. But does she know he may have hurt her? Left her lying on the shore. Was it the wee seal – did he go to kill it? After my phone call.

They say it all depends on tides and currents. The body might be thrown up on Jura or Scarba. Maybe that's what he wanted – the dark inside to be sucked down. God help him.

Out here the weather's pretending nothing ever happened. Blue skies like a week past; gentle clouds breezing over the wreckage. Coming down the path, Eilean na Cleirich looks new minted. Bird life back in business. No trace of errant seals.

Shame about the bodies. Maybe we're going to wake up soon.

The beach brings it right back though. Flotsam everywhere. Beacons tumbled amidst the rest. But above the tideline, a big four by four is drawn up at the cave, with the complete contents of Lucy's camp laid out for serious packing.

He's a big, bearded guy, Ian, all shaggy hair and earnest geniality. Lucy barely reaches his shoulder with her fine boned elegance. They look great together.

Getting down to the introductions, it's not the easy wind-down we imagined.

'Poor Bridget.'

'Donald's gone as well. They're not sure of finding him.'

I didn't flag the detail. What else was there to say? So, I helped Ian with his loading. We exchanged phone numbers and e-mails. Promised to be at the preview, whatever the posting might be.

That was it. Last hug. Handshake. The truce was over, sanctuary breached.

I climb slowly back to Well Croft and my own waiting car. Reports will be written; the place remains.

LONG AND SHALLOW *and far away; unrolling like a map.*

On one side run narrow straits of sea. Wind crested. On the other, sea loch reaches like an extended finger. Making almost an island.

At the top there is a village and sheltered harbour. And to the west on the sea side, a landing place.

Below that a wide sandy bay extends, closed off at the southern end by a rocky arm that points seaward. And in that bay an island. Sanctuary Bay. Beyond the arm, on both sides, stony shorelines run below rough muirland.

Once the roads were all at sea; this peninsula, the landfall.

No-one has to come this way now, but sanctuary waits still on strangers.

Luath Press Limited

committed to publishing well written books worth reading

LUATH PRESS takes its name from Robert Burns, whose little collie Luath (*Gael.*, swift or nimble) tripped up Jean Armour at a wedding and gave him the chance to speak to the woman who was to be his wife and the abiding love of his life. Burns called one of the 'Twa Dogs' Luath after Cuchullin's hunting dog in Ossian's *Fingal*. Luath Press was established in 1981 in the heart of Burns country, and is now based a few steps up the road from Burns' first lodgings on Edinburgh's Royal Mile. Luath offers you distinctive writing with a hint of unexpected pleasures.

Most bookshops in the UK, the US, Canada, Australia, New Zealand and parts of Europe, either carry our books in stock or can order them for you. To order direct from us, please send a £sterling cheque, postal order, international money order or your credit card details (number, address of cardholder and expiry date) to us at the address below. Please add post and packing as follows: UK – £1.00 per delivery address; overseas surface mail – £2.50 per delivery address; overseas airmail – £3.50 for the first book to each delivery address, plus £1.00 for each additional book by airmail to the same address. If your order is a gift, we will happily enclose your card or message at no extra charge.

Luath Press Limited
543/2 Castlehill
The Royal Mile
Edinburgh EH1 2ND
Scotland
Telephone: +44 (0)131 225 4326 (24 hours)
Email: sales@luath.co.uk
Website: www.luath.co.uk